A tale from The House of the Human

Mara

and the

Magic Sketchbook

by JP Goorjian

Mara and the Magic Sketchbook is a work of fiction. Names, characters, places and incidents either are the product of the author's imagination or are used fictitiously. Any resemblance to actual persons, living or dead, events or locales is entirely coincidental.

2020 Paperback Edition

Copyright © 2020 by John-Paul Goorjian

Published by John-Paul Goorjian

paperback ISBN 978-1-7352660-3-9

ebook ISBN 978-1-7352660-7-7

Cover Design by Leticia Ramirez. Copyright © 2020

John-Paul Goorjian: www.wizard.vip, @jpgoorjian
Leticia Ramiriez: @leticiagravitania

THANK YOU

Huge hugs to Auntie Mary, who journeyed onward to another plane of existence some time back. She is one of the most colorful creative persons that I have had the privilege of spending time with. Everything in her house spoke of her joy for living and for our beautiful planet and for the amazing culture we humans have created the world over.

Thank you to my mother Joanne and my father Paul for always telling me that I was capable of anything that I could dream of. Thank you to my sister Taline, whose smile and whose joy and kindness has inspired both me and anyone who is fortunate to meet her.

Thank you to my cousin Mike, who has helped me to become the author that I am. He has believed in me, encouraged me, inspired me, and pushed me to find excellence in every thread of story that I weave.

Thank you to Leticia for doing such an amazing job on the cover design. She has continually inspired me with her art and her passion for creation. She has rekindled my fire when the rain has poured more times than I can remember.

Thank you to my amazing friends Jeff and Josh, who I've known forever and who have always cheered me on and offered me the honest guidance of true friends.

Thank you to my wife, Snowma, who makes every day of my life delightful. She makes me look forward to the future, nostalgic for the past, and grateful for the present.

And finally, big huge thanks to you, the reader, for giving me a chance to be an author.

Note to Reader:

If you don't know what a word means, then look it up.

Wisdom is to know when you don't know.

MARA

AND

THE

MAGIC
SKETCHBOOK

Chapter 1: Origin

The fate of Mara's spaceship depends upon her next choice —bumble bees or pigeons?

She scrunches her eyes and imagines a race between the two. The bumble bee totally ditches the pigeon. Bumble bees would make her spaceship go way faster. Way faster.

Outside her classroom window, the real pigeon is still on the picnic table bobbing its head, but the bumble bee by the bush flew away. Mara drums her fingers on the desk.

"Hey! Mara! Quit drifting off!" Mr Jones, the sixth grade teacher shakes his pen at her.

The first page of the lesson has all sorts of weird blobs on it.

Mr. Jones writes 'EVOLUTION' on the board. "We *evolved* from microscopic creatures..."

Mara slips her sketchbook out and draws more flowers into the roots of her plant spaceship. The bees are gonna need them.

Auntie's gonna love this sketchbook. It's full of outer space monsters, googly aliens and crazy planets. Mara's got a whole shelf of sketchbooks to show Auntie, whenever she comes back.

Mr. Jones drones on, "After the dinosaurs, fossils indicate

that humans *evolved* from primates..."

Mara's only got her favorite purple pencil, but the flowers are supposed to be lots of different colors. She draws in the little bees whose buzzing wings are gonna make her ship go super fast.

"Mara! Can you please put your sketchbook away!" Mr. Jones suddenly says.

Mara shrinks as the class looks at her again. She slides her sketchbook back into her desk.

"History got us here. History shows us where we need to go," Mr Jones says.

Cal, another kid from the back row, shouts, "You need to go to la la land little Miss Scribbles."

"Don't call me that!" Mara shouts back and laser beams him with her eyes.

"Miss scribbles!"

Mara spins towards the window and frowns.

Mr. Jones raises his voice, "Cal! None of that now. Okay class, quiet down and look at the farm in your lesson. He writes 'AGRICULTURE' on the board.

Mara's gonna draw some veggies into the branches of her spaceship. She bites her lip. Maybe Auntie won't even like her drawings. Maybe they are just scribbles.

That pigeon is still standing on the picnic table bobbing its head at her. Weirdo pigeon.

Mr. Jones is talking about, "... sailing ships let us explore the world. Turn the page."

There's a spinning wheel, a steam engine, a computer and a spaceship

The sun glints off the window. The pigeon's beak opens and closes as it quietly coos.

Mara rubs her eyes. Everyone's so interested in class.

Then, suddenly,

Tak! Tak! Tak!

Mara jumps in her seat.

Tak! Tak! Tak!

The pigeon bangs on the window. It waves at her with its wing.

"Uh..." Mara says.

Her classmates all stare at the board.

"Guys?" she whispers, but strangely, no one hears her. She closes her eyes really tight.

Tak! Tak!

"What're you doing?" Mara asks the bird.

The pigeon tries to open the window with its wings. It strains super hard, then gives up and glares at her.

Mara leans over and cracks open the window. But the pigeon shakes its head and holds its wings up higher. So she quickly stands and opens the window all the way, then she drops back into her seat and stares at the lesson.

Mr. Jones underlines the word 'EVOLUTION.'

The pigeon puts its wings on its hips and cocks its head to the side.

"Are you for real?" Mara whispers.

It rolls its eyes, then hops through the window and holds its leg up. There's a note tied around it.

"Uh..." Mara reaches forward and unties the slip of paper.

It's just the tiniest little note. Handwriting she knows like her own.

Mara, I need your help. Come quickly! Love, Auntie.

"Oh no," Mara whispers. The pigeon backs out through the window and waves for her to follow.

"What?" she asks.

The pigeon stomps its foot, then swoops its wing in a big curve.

"You want me to climb out the window?"

The pigeon bobs its head furiously.

Her class is totally absorbed in the lesson.

Mara stuffs her sketchbook, pencil, and the little note, into the front pocket of her overalls. Then she slowly stands and leans towards the window, until she slides out and tumbles behind the bushes.

No one noticed. Mara pinches her finger.

"Coo coo." The pigeon waves at her from the picnic table.

She crawls under the bushes towards it, then she hops up and chases after the bird as it flies ahead. It waves her onwards until it flits down and lands on the handlebars of her bike.

"I hope you're taking me to Auntie," Mara says as she gets on and flips up the kickstand.

Then the pigeon flies, and Mara follows faster and faster until her hair flows behind her and the pedals are a blur. Out of the city and up into the redwoods, she races after the bird, careening past cars along the skyline. The tall trees flash by in burgundy and green. The little bird swoops over the top of the mountain and following close, Mara crests the ridge and sweeps down the bendy curves to the canyon floor. Faster and faster on the straightaway, the oak and maple leaves whip in her wake.

Finally, the pigeon veers off the pavement and they take a little unmarked dirt road deep into the woods.

After a ways, the bird flies down and lands, causing Mara to skid to a stop.

Ahead, the road curves behind the trees.

The pigeon taps on the bike, flutters up a few inches into the air and gestures to the ground. Mara kicks down the kickstand and parks her bike. Now the bird lands, points down the road, then tip-toes in a circle with one feather over its beak.

"I'll be real careful," Mara whispers.

The bird bobs its head and coos. It looks away, takes a few random steps, and starts pecking around for bugs.

Mara reaches up to her front pocket and touches her sketchbook. Auntie's gonna love her drawings, she won't call them scribbles. There's no way she's gonna call them scribbles. Mara hates Miss Scribbles!

She stomps forward.

"Coo coo," the pigeon calls.

"Oh right." Mara shakes it off and gives the pigeon a thumbs up.

Then she tiptoes down the road, around the curve, all the way to the end, where a long row of gold painted cars with tinted windows are parked.

Gaudy. That's what Auntie would call those cars. Mara moves past the gaudy vehicles to a wall of piled black stones at the end of the road. As she approaches the rock wall, it sparkles like starlight in the way that Auntie loves. Mara knows she's on the right track, but there's no house on the other side, just a freshly hacked path into the woods.

She frowns. There's supposed to be a house on the other side of the wall! And there's supposed to be a gate in the wall! And Auntie's supposed to be opening the gate and Mara's supposed to be running into her arms for a great big hug! That's how it's always been. At all of Auntie's houses.

The oaks rustle, and their branches scratch against each other.

Mara pulls out the tiny note and traces her aunt's writing with her finger. *Mara, I need your help.*

Mara looks into the woods beyond. Then she tucks the note into her sketchbook and snaps her front pocket closed.

There's litter on the ground next to the cars. "Hmm." Friends of Auntie would never throw trash on the ground.

Mara's gonna find out what's going on here, and she's gonna save Auntie.

Chapter 2: Evolution

Mara climbs over the sparkly rock wall and hops down to the forest floor on the other side. It smells like hacked-up vegetation. Whoever these gaudy people are, they just chopped their way through the oaks and huckleberries.

Mara tip-toes forward and makes her way into the woods. After a short distance, the path becomes soggy and Mara's foot suddenly sticks. She throws her arms forward to catch herself, but her arms and face go right down into a murky pool. In the water, she's somehow able to see millions of microscopic creatures battling over a fine leather glove that some woman dropped. Mara scrambles up from the bank, shakes her hair and wipes the water from her eyes. "Blobs, and a really gaudy glove," she says to herself. "A greedy glove."

Mara's whole take on clothing is to keep it simple and useful, thus the overalls. She's always liked pretty stitching though.

"Oh wow!" She notices that the pool she fell in is actually a narrow moat that runs in both directions. On its surface, the dust and leaves float without moving in a way that makes the water blend right in with the forest floor.

The moat isn't wide, so she hops right over, but she's only able to take a few steps before a growling roar off to her left rumbles through the trees. A shudder of terror runs through Mara. The roar is followed by stomping and crashing and more roaring and hooting and the trees begin to shake. Mara dashes behind an oak tree.

Instead of the herd of crazy wild animals she was expecting, two T-Rex dinosaurs appear. They're roaring and their eyes are huge and they're running full speed right at her.

Mara's hair stands on its ends. She bolts—sprints down the path, so fast it feels like she's in front of herself. The T-Rexes storm closer. They chomp their teeth and wave their arms. They pound and shake the forest.

Mara runs faster than she ever has before. She feels tiny and huge at the same time, like a floating bubble with arms and legs that are spinning. But the T-Rexes are way bigger. They're gonna catch her. She's gonna get eaten! She doesn't want to get eaten!

But then, the T-Rexes charge right past her. They're actually only about twice as tall as Mara, and they keep looking over their shoulders, looking past her.

Behind her, Mara hears an even louder crashing and hooting and screeching. She glances back, then almost falls over forward as she launches into rocket mode to catch up with the T-Rexes.

Hundreds of primates surge through the forest chasing her.

They swing through the branches and bounce off the tree trunks. They shriek and pound their chests.

"Ahhh!" Mara shouts.

A flash of yellow zips past Mara's head. Then another, and another. Bananas! The primates wildly fling bananas! The T-rexes ahead of her try to cover their big heads with their little arms, yelping as they dodge the fruit.

Mara shields her face racing to get away. Bananas are flying all around her! An accurate banana slams into her arm. The fruit explodes and splatters all over. "Aaah!" she yells, wiping at her eyes.

The hooting and screeching is right behind her now. And in her path, a mushy banana awaits. Still trying to clear her eyes, she steps right on it and starts sliding along on the peel! Her arms windmill out of control.

But then, right in front of her, a big hairy caveman leaps out of the bushes and yells, "Everybody freeze!"

The T-Rexes skid into each other and fall. Mara slides past them. The primates all crash and splash, piling up in the pathway. The caveman swoops over, catches Mara's hand, and then swings her up in the air, and around, and lands her on her feet.

"You okay?" he asks her with a slow, deep voice. He's really really hairy, and he wears a bearskin around his waist and over his shoulder.

The T-Rexes climb back to their feet, and start to wipe the leaves off their chests. Everywhere else, the primates whimper and

9

glance at the caveman. Some pick fleas out of their neighbor's fur.

"Yeah, I guess so," Mara says.

The caveman yells to the primates, "Hey! Rex brothers not mess trees. Bad people mess trees. You say sorry!" But then he whispers to Mara, "You not bad people?"

"No!" she says. "I'm just trying to find my aunt."

The Rex brothers get the last of the leaves off each other's backs as one of the older primates comes over and hands each of them a banana.

"Good," the caveman says as they make peace. Then he whispers again to Mara, "Auntie in big trouble. Really scary bad people here."

Mara frowns when she hears that.

Suddenly the leaves of the tree next to them rustle and a girl hops down. She's a bit taller than Mara, slightly older, hair wrapped up with a stick, and she's got really intense eyes. Her clothes are simple, Mara likes them. But she's just covered in mud and clay, like a ghostly patch of mottled earth, like a wild jungle girl. She's pretty scary. Mara sidles closer to the caveman.

The girl points at Mara. "Who's this Kreak?"

"Nice girl, looks for Auntie. What name nice girl?"

"Mara."

"I Kreak." He shakes her hand. "Sarah, Mara." Then he chuckles. "Name sound same!"

Sarah looks at Mara's overalls. "Auntie needs warriors."

Mara lets go of Kreak's hand. "I'm a... Um... I can help!

Auntie sent me a note."

Sarah humfs. "Kreak, we need to go set those traps."

But just then, a massive explosion thunders through the forest.

"Holy moly!" Sarah yells as they all drop to the ground. The Rex brothers take off and the primates dash in all directions.

Kreak jumps back to his feet. "Auntie!" he yells

Sarah hops up also. "Come on, we gotta…"

Mara's already running straight towards the horrible sound.

"Hey wait!" Sarah yells. "Come on Kreak!"

They catch up to Mara and Kreak takes the lead.

"This way," he says and turns onto an animal trail. "Fast!" Kreak yells.

Sarah's quick as a deer, and Mara runs hard to keep up. They run until the trees become a whirlwind of shapes and figures.

Finally they burst out of the woods into tall grass. Kreak stops so fast that Sarah runs right into him, and Mara runs right into her. Kreak barely budges as they bounce off of him.

"Oooof," Sarah says.

"Ow." Mara rubs her forehead.

Kreak points across the field at two heavy wooden doors that are set into a towering rock wall which blocks the entire view ahead. "Auntie!"

"That's Auntie's house?" Mara asks.

"Garden!" Kreak yells.

Sarah shushes him, "Be quiet Kreak. The bad guys might

be right on the other side."

Kreak cringes, then whispers, "Auntie garden."

"My tiny house is in the garden," Sarah adds. Then she leads them quietly across through the grass towards the heavy old doors in the massive wall of giant stones.

The doors are made of split logs, thick with moss, and are as rough and wild as the jagged wall they go through. They're open just a bit.

And on the other side, it sounds like Niagara Falls.

Chapter 3: Agriculture

Sarah pushes the mossy doors open a little more, then Mara and Kreak follow her through.

A huge river is raging and storming through the garden.

"HOLY MOLY! My house!" Sarah exclaims. But at the same time, Kreak hisses and points across the river, "Bad people!"

The three of them jump behind some bushes.

Auntie's garden is pretty big. It's encompassed by the massive rock wall that they're crouched near. The wall horseshoes around and connects with both of its ends to the steep hillside across from them. But in the wall, far to their left, is a big jagged hole where water crashes through and feeds this massive river. The river roars across the gardens. Ripped up plants and broken branches churn in the water's fury.

And across the river, all the way across the garden from them, is a mean-looking army of bad people. The army is gathered in front of an arched doorway that leads directly into the steep hillside beyond.

"Wow," Mara says.

"They've totally ruined the gardens," Sarah whispers. "And see Kreak, I told you it was a whole army."

"Is that the front door to Auntie's house? Mara asks.

"Ya," Sara says.

"The front door leads into the mountain?"

"Ya," Sarah says again.

The three of them watch as a technician type from the army kneels before the front door. More techs wait with their gear. Soldiers types with collared tee-shirts and gadgets on their belts stand ready. Some of them scan the garden. In the center of the army, a small group of people that Mara thinks are the leaders, wear silk and leather suits, and jewelry that gleams in the sun. They've got gaudy things like umbrellas, canes, small bags, and fancy sunglasses.

But mostly, Mara is still thinking about how the front door leads into the hillside. "Auntie's house is in the mountain?" she asks with wonder.

"I guess so," Sarah says. "I've just been inside the greeting room there."

"Wow," Mara says again.

The technician finally cracks the door, then backs away and a group of soldiers stream in. The finely dressed group continues to chat with each other until one of the soldiers ducks their head back out and gives the thumbs up.

The rest of the small army heads inside, then Mara asks, "What do they want?"

"Auntie," Kreak sighs.

"We think they want to kidnap her." Sarah says.

"No!" Mara cries out when she hears that. She jumps up. "Come on!"

"Wait! River." Kreak says.

"Ya," Sarah shakes her head. "I don't think we can cross." She points to the wall off to their left, "They blew the dam to bits. I figure the lake will take maybe a day or so to empty."

Mara's eyebrows tighten. "We can't wait that long."

"You wanna swim across that madness?" Sarah asks.

Mara shakes her head, "I was thinking we could make a fork in it."

"You're crazy." Sarah scoffs and rolls her eyes at Mara.

"Hey!" Kreak pushes Sarah a little.

"Oh come on Kreak, That river's like a hundred feet wide."

"Look." Mara pulls out her sketchbook and pencil and quickly sketches the garden. "Okay here's the garden. And the river. But see over there is that big ditch. And look, this part of the river bank is keeping the water from the ditch."

Sarah cuts in, "And the ditch leads to that huge grate in the wall. Okay, you're pretty good at drawing, but how do we move the river bank?"

Mara shrugs. "That's what I'm not sure about. Dig through it somehow…? I was still thinking about that part."

"What a great idea!" Sarah says sarcastically and turns away towards the river putting her hands on her hips.

Mara frowns. This is exactly why she doesn't show anyone her art. And this isn't even her idea. It's cause Mr. Jones said something about agriculture. Really great. Really original. Mara spins her pencil around and grinds her eraser into the river bank she drew. She growls and erases every last bit of it. Then she spins her pencil back around and creates waves and froth and then she steers the river down the ditch. She furiously shadows and shades. The river in her drawing pours out the gate. Finished, Mara whips her pencil away from the sketchbook.

But as she finishes her drawing, something happens that's never, ever happened before. As she spins her pencil away, her drawing suddenly flares with brilliant purple light! And then sparks, purple sparks begin to dance across the page, across the lines she's drawn. They stream through her drawing of the garden and into the river. The sparks seem to gather into the part of the drawing she's changed and then they bounce off the page. The sparks fill the air, swirling around her. Mara gasps.

"Holy moly Mara!" Sarah yells.

Kreak runs over at first, but then cowers back as the light around Mara intensifies. Her drawing seems to be shaping the streams of purple sparks that are flowing from her sketchbook.

"I don't know what's happening!" Mara shouts. "I don't know... Oh look!" She points at the river.

The real river yells, and then it surges towards the bank blocking the ditch. The river crashes and rips. Dirt spits in huge fountains of brown clods and splatters the trees. The river serpents and chomps and chews with frothy white teeth. And then it roars and rears itself high into the air and with a huge blast, it slams itself though the bank. Unleashed, the river races down the ditch and charges through the grate of freedom.

"Holy moly!" Sarah looks back at Mara. "Did you just draw…?"

"Ya," Mara whispers as the last of the purple sparks blink away. She closes her sketchbook and clutches it to the front of her overalls. *Did I really just make that happen? Did I make that happen with my drawing?* she thinks to herself. Her heart is beating so fast. Mara bites her lip.

Sarah watches Mara as she slides her sketchbook into her front pocket. Then Sarah glances at her own hands. She turns away towards the river and watches it shrink itself back down. Finally she says,"Well, we can cross now."

Kreak helps Mara to her feet and they follow Sarah down to the water.

They make their way through the mud and torn up plants that are left in the wake of the receding river. The river has shrunken now to the point where it looks easy to cross.

Sarah jumps between four broken posts that are sticking up out of the churned up mud. "This is my house."

"Oh, no," Mara says.

"Ya." Sarah frowns. "But we got bigger fish to catch," and she wades into the river a few steps. "Current's not too bad. Mara, your sketchbook."

"Oh, it's okay, Auntie gave me this. It never gets messed up."

"Oh. Uhh, okay," Sarah says and moves deeper. "How's that work? How'd you do that with the river?"

Mara shakes her head. "I don't know." She was so angry when she was drawing. She's so sick of people making fun of her ideas. She waves her fingers through the water and shivers a bit.

Sarah's a little taller than her, but they both hold Kreak's hands through the deepest part.

After climbing out of the river, they shake the water off and take position behind some bushes a short distance from the front door that leads into the mountain.

Mara can see that the door is made of slats of wood which have greyed in the sun. Near the top, a stained-glass depiction of Earth sparkles in the sun. And around the door, on either side and above, the green hillside rises, covered in colonies of white and pink wildflowers. The grass flickers against the door's frame in the gentle breeze.

Kreak gently brushes away a bumble bee.

"The greeting room is through there?" Mara asks in a whisper.

"Ya," Sarah nods. "Do you think we should just open it?"

"Bad people," Kreak warns.

"We've gotta try," Sarah says, and without waiting for an answer, she tiptoes right up to the door.

Mara watches, ready to rush forward, while Kreak bobs up and down with his fists clenched.

Sarah glances back at them, then she reaches for the door

knob and gently, gently turns it. The door cracks open and Sarah springs back behind and hides.

No one comes out.

After a moment, a little breeze pushes the door open a little more.

Sarah creeps back and peeks through. Then she waves Mara and Kreak over, and the three of them head through the door into Auntie's house.

Right when she enters her aunt's house, Mara grins really big. The greeting room smells just like all of Auntie's houses when you step in the front door. Wild rose potpourri.

The ceiling flows up and away from the front door with the rising of the hillside. Several other doors are in the side walls, but there is a big one, directly across from them, that's very grand. It's made of swirled and spotted burlwood. Shelves are everywhere else. The shelves are covered with the little artifacts and books that Auntie loves to collect. Chairs with flowery fabric cozy up to small tables, and there's also a large pile of sitting pillows in the corner. The pile goes almost to the ceiling which Mara thinks is a lot strange.

Kreak stands with his mouth open looking at the tea sets, the tiny cars, the gumby dolls, there's all sorts of things on the shelves.

"I have lemonade with Auntie in here," Sarah says.

"That sounds really nice." Mara says. She tries to remember what Auntie's lemonade tastes like, but she can't.

"Auntie's lemonade is the be..What's that?!" Sarah suddenly cries out.

The huge pile of pillows against the wall starts to shake and quake and grunt. It honks and hops towards them. Kreak and the two girls run behind a chair.

Then the pile starts shooting pillows out. One hits Kreak right in the face! "Ruuunn!" he hollers and bolts outside.

"Wait Kreak..." Sarah says as she darts forward. She dodges a few flyers, then slides the last few feet to the quaking mound of pillows. She dives into the pile. She rips and tears at it, flinging pillows in all directions. Frenzied, tearing the pile to bits, she finally cries out, "I thought so! You guys it's Doctor Zhao!"

The last of the pillows bounce off the walls and settle.

Kreak peeks back in.

Mara pushes some pillows out of her way and crawls out from under a chair.

Doctor Zhao is all tied up and twisted! Mara rushes over. She's never seen someone tied up before, it looks terribly uncomfortable. She quickly helps Sarah to untie him.

"Oh my goodness!" Doctor Zhao gasps for air as they remove his gag.

"Are you okay?" Sarah and Mara both ask.

"Yes, but my breath… I need to catch my breath."

Kreak joins them and the three finish untying the ropes from Doctor Zhao's wrists and ankles. The older man gets to his feet and takes a few deep breaths to calm himself. Then he gently smooths the wrinkles out of his burgundy suit with his hands. He straightens the watch chain across his vest. And after a good harrumph, he finally says, "Well thank you all very much, that was extremely uncomfortable. Sarah, Kreak, I'm so glad you're safe. And you must be Mara. It's good to finally meet you. I am Doctor Zhao."

"The Director of Operations for the House," Sarah adds.

Mara shakes his hand. "It's nice to meet you Doctor Zhao. But how do you know who I am?"

"I've seen pictures of you in The Designer's various offices," he says.

"The Designer?"

"Oh! I'm sorry, yes, your aunt is called The Design..."

"Is she okay?" Mara blurts out.

Doctor Zhao furrows his brow, but then pats her on the shoulder and says, "We're gonna find her." He checks his watch. "Quickly though Mara, how did you get here?"

"Well, I guess um... well, a very strange pigeon came to my class with a note from Auntie. Then the pigeon led me here."

"Hmm, that is strange. Could I see the note?"

She pulls it out of her sketchbook and gives it to him.

He raises an eyebrow while he reads the note. "Hmm..." He looks curiously at Mara while he hands the note back to her. "I see you've got one of The Designer's journals there."

Mara pushes her sketchbook back into her front pocket, then snaps it closed. "This is one of my sketchbooks. Auntie gave them to me."

"Oh, of course. Well, The Designer, your aunt, I'm hoping that she's gotten to safety. Even though the house is much bigger than she planned it to be, she is the one who designed it."

"Bigger than she planned it to be? Um, can we go to her?" Mara takes a few steps towards the grand burlwood door.

"Hold on Mara!" Doctor Zhao raises his hands. "These are nefarious invaders. They had me tied, trussed and buried in pillows in the time it would take to pour a cup of tea. We can't just charge ahead."

"Okay," Mara says. "I'll follow you."

"Okay, good. Thank you. Now I didn't get a good look at them—regardless, our best bet is to try and find your aunt. Look, if we can make it to my office, there's a map and a phone."

Mara nods. "Okay."

"Sarah, Kreak, you coming?" Doctor Zhao asks.

"Ya," Sarah says, and Kreak nods furiously.

Doctor Zhao nods. "Good. Okay now, slowly and cautiously, yes?"

"Slowly and cautiously," Mara says.

"Good." Doctor Zhao crosses to the burlwood door, holds the handle of the door for a few moments, and then opens it.

"Oh my," he says.

The hallway is darker than a tomb.

Chapter 4: Identity

The light from the greeting room meekly spills through the door into the hallway. It is pitch black. All of the light fixtures in the hall are smashed, and fragments of glass on the carpet sharply reflect the light.

"Got a flashlight?" Mara asks.

"No." Doctor Zhao shakes his head.

"Let's hold hands," she says.

"Good idea." He nods and they form a chain. "Slow and cautious," he says as he leads them in. "I'll try to kick the glass out of the way, but shuffle your feet. We need to make it quite a ways down this hallway." He touches a wall with one hand and holds Mara's with the other. Sarah follows, then Kreak.

They slowly move past one door, then another, then a third, and finally the hallway turns to the right and the last scrap of light winks out. They're in total darkness.

"Um…" Doctor Zhao says. "Seems like we're doing all right. So in about twenty feet we'll head through the middle passageway."

"This is pretty scary," Sarah says.

Mara hates it, she can't see anything. It's like being in the middle of nothing.

But then, a horrible cackle sounds out from directly above them. Mara and her friends instantly freeze.

"What was that?" Mara whispers. Kreak whimpers slightly.

Then a different voice from above, a big deep one, says, "You dolt, they heard you! Just pull it will ya?"

That horrible laugh again, and a net suddenly springs up around Mara, Sarah and Kreak. It misses Doctor Zhao though, who gets knocked back. Everyone is hollering as the net gets pulled up in a tangle through the ceiling.

Doctor Zhao jumps around in the darkness. "No, no! Oh my goodness!"

Mara screams, "Run Doctor Zhao!"

"No! Okay. I'll find you!" Doctor Zhao yells back, then he bolts away down the hall.

The three of them in the net get pulled all the way through the ceiling to the next level. And then, like a sack, they get slung over the shoulder of an absolutely massive human. Kreak and Sarah try to punch and kick at him through the net, but he ignores them. Mara curls up tight around her sketchbook. *This is horrible. We're captured already,* she thinks to herself grimly.

"Come on Chawz," the big man says in his deep voice.

"Ya, we got em!" his sidekick laughs. "We got em, we got em, we got em!"

Out of the dark room, Mara, Sarah and Kreak are carried through a series of stone hallways until they turn into some sort of

24

little chapel. Rows of wooden pews face a raised dais with a simple table on it. The massive human carries them to the front of the room and then spills them onto the floor.

"Ooof." "Ow!' "Hey!" Sarah and Kreak untangle themselves from each other. Mara uncurls and hops out of their way.

"I'm Carl," the giant human says and sits down on the front pew which he almost fills. Carl tugs on his suspenders and lets them snap against his short sleeved floral shirt. Then he taps his sidekick, a tall boy in jeans and a dirty t-shirt. "This is Chawz."

The boy giggles. "Hey stupids!"

Mara crumples her nose. Bullies. She hates bullies.

Sarah makes it to her feet and whips around, "You're stupid!"

"Sarah!" Mara whispers.

Kreak pulls the last bit of net over his head and roars. "Bad people!"

"Hold on!" Carl booms and makes a fist. Then he points at Sarah and Kreak. "You two look like natives." He shifts to Mara. "You, not so much though."

"I'm Mara." She takes a step forward and points at him. "You guys are bullies!"

Carl chuckles. "Mara, very nice to meet you."

"Where's my aunt? Did you take her? You need to leave her house!"

"Shut up!" Chawz squeals.

"Her house?" Carl laughs. "What a house, eh Chawz?"

Chawz smirks and snorts until Carl baps him on the head. "So now Mara, you came to see your aunt, but she's got some visitors, ya?"

"BAD PEOPLE!" Kreak yells shaking his fists over his head.

Carl grabs Chawz and hurls the boy at Kreak. Kreak tries to dodge, but Chawz missiles feet first into him and kicks him across the room. Chawz rolls to his feet screeching with laughter.

"Holy moly!" Sarah yells.

Mara screams, "Stop it!" and runs over to Kreak. She stands with her arms out in front of her. "Are you all right?" she says over her shoulder.

Kreak pushes himself back to his feet, and with his hands over his stomach, he whispers into Mara's ear, "Bad people."

"You know Chawz," Carl stands up. "I'll bet our bosses captured The Designer already, so why don'ts we take these three to see her right now." He chuckles. "We'll reunite you with your Auntie, Mara, and thens we can all watch the plan get executed."

Mara's lips snarl. She'll never let the plan get executed!

"You need to relax little one." Carl points at her. He stands up and stretches his arms out, almost filling the room, then says, "You guys wanna be tied up and carried, or you's gonna just come along all nice?"

They answer all at once:

Mara scrunches her face up really tight and says, "Please

take us to Auntie."

While Kreak holds up his hands. "Don't throw people."

And Sarah says, "I'm not gonna fight you!"

"Great," Carl says. And he grabs Sarah by the back of her shirt and Kreak by the back of his bear skin, then he walks them out of the chapel. Chawz grabs Mara's elbow and pushes her along.

Mara frowns, then raises an eyebrow. What if she could do that thing again with her sketchbook? Maybe she could sneak it out and draw something.

Something to trip them, ya.

Like... bananas.

Bananas? Oh come on, if she gonna help Auntie she's gotta have more original ideas. Mara glares at Carl's back.

They pass into a wide, grey, stone hallway. Carl fills it up. But he also walks fast, so Chawz keeps shoving Mara to keep up. He's such a bully.

High up near the ceiling, some daylight streams in through stained glass windows. The colored light plays over the walls and the floor. Even Chawz is hushed by its beauty.

Then there's a click. And the large flagstone Mara's walking on swings open.

"Whoa!" she yells as she falls into the trapdoor.

Chawz, who's firmly gripping her arm, is pulled through also. "Dangit! AHHHHH!" he screams. The two begin to slide down into the darkness. Above them, the flagstone slams shut and closes out the light completely.

They slide faster and faster. Above, Carl's bellows and stomps fade into the distance. Mara tries to shake Chawz off. "You're hurting me!"

"Sorry," he says and relaxes his grip on her arm. "I'm scared."

"Me too," Mara says. She checks the snap on her front pocket. "Just try to calm down."

They slide down ramps and around spirals, Chawz clings to her. He snorts and squeals like a goat. Mara just holds her arms across her chest and closes her eyes. Her face is drawn tight.

Worst.

Slide.

Ever.

And then the two suddenly drop through the ceiling of a room and splash into a well of water.

They bob back up to the surface and latch onto the edge of the round well. They catch their breath for a moment, then they crawl out of the water and flop onto the stone floor of the subterranean room.

Eventually Mara gets to her feet and scans the room. It's the creepiest room she's ever been in. A huge rectangular stone room, four rows of large square columns obscure the far corners, and it seems empty except for the well. On the far wall, all the way across from them, are double doors leading out. And then there's the chandelier.

28

She takes a few steps towards the creeping fixture. It fits the room, or rather, the room fits the chandelier. It seems to grow out of cracks in the center of the ceiling. Branches twine down and sprawl out into viney extensions that terminate in clusters of tiny bright lights. The chandelier weaves around, it shines in corners and reaches behind columns.

Chawz gets to his feet. "That's some kinda chandelier there, eh?" He nudges Mara with his elbow. "Now don't get stupid on me. You're still my prisoner."

"Fine, I'm still your prisoner, but I want you to help me find my aunt," she whispers.

"Sure," Chawz says. "This room feels weird." He moves to a nearby column and looks around it. Then he gasps in terror, barely able to whisper, "What's tha...?" He backs up slowly.

"What?" Mara whispers.

"Shu...." Chawz freezes.

Mara moves sideways a few steps. "What's there?" She takes a few more. But she doesn't see anything behind the column. "Chawz?"

"He..." Chawz's eyes are wide with fear, and fixed straight ahead of him. "Can't you see him?" he squawks.

"Who?" Mara whispers. There's no one there.

"Me...it's me..." Chawz groans. He starts to shake.

Then Mara sees someone. She gasps. She sees someone on the other side of the room. No one was there a second ago. She was just looking there! It's a girl, the same age as her, standing with arms crossed between one of the columns and the far wall. Mara can hear the girl's whispers crawling across the room, but she can't see who the girl is talking to.

Mara tiptoes closer and hides behind a column. She can hear the girl now. She's got a sharp voice. "I told you to let me do the drawing, but no! And look what happened. I mean, how lame are you? I think you should..."

The girl keeps going on like this,and Mara's skin crawls. There's something about the voice. But then a new noise startles her. She leans around the other edge of the column.

Another girl! She's come through the double doors and is shambling slowly down the center of the room. Her shoulders are slumped, her head, stooped.

Mara draws in a quick breath. Her stomach rolls. She dashes behind another column. She's so terrified. She can feel her heart thumping against her sketchbook.

The new girl shuffles closer, muttering, "Stupid garbage. Horrible ideas. I wish they'd just leave me alone cause I hate em. I just hate em all..."

Mara's heart clogs her throat. That voice. She tries to see the girl's face, but the girl's greasy hair hangs in the way.

Suddenly, another girl! She just appears in front of Mara. Mara recoils into the column, and clutches her sketchbook. This new girl, her back is turned and her head is held very high. It's like she's talking to a whole group of people who aren't there. And her voice, her voice!

Mara's breath stops. A silent scream tears through her—she realizes now—that girl has her voice! And the other ones, they have her voice too!

"Yes. So true. I mean, I did that drawing before the one we're talking about now. Oh yes. It won lots of awards. It won all the awards...." Mara's own voice boasts.

Then the shambling girl passes close. "They said my art is horrible. They said I'm not creative at all. They don't like me. Nobody likes me..."

The girl's greasy hair swings to the side and her chin comes into view. *No!* Mara pushes away from the column and tries to get to Chawz.

The shambling girl shakes her head, and as her hair swings out of the way, "No!" Mara yells out loud this time. She stumbles back and falls to the ground. "No!" she gasps, trembling.

The girl has her face! It's Mara! That person is Mara!

More girls appear. Mara's eyes dart from one to the next. They're all different, but they're all her, slightly different versions of her.

"You're not creative."

"I'm the prettiest."

"Everyone hates me."

Tears well in Mara's eyes. Everything gets blurry. In a panic, she wipes at her face and crawls towards Chawz. More girls are appearing. Girls that stand like her, that talk like her. Some are horrible, some normal, a few seem kind.

Chawz is babbling on his knees. He's looking everywhere at once.

"Chawz…" Mara tries to whisper. She's shaking.

Chawz jumps at her voice. He stares at her for a moment, trying to recognize her. Then he bursts out, "Mara! Do you see them? Do you see them?" Mara reaches out to him. Chawz grabs her arm and they huddle close. "Do you see them?" he asks.

"Yes. Yes, I see them," Mara whispers.

But Chawz isn't seeing the Maras that Mara sees. "Chawz, what, what do you see?"

"It's me," Chawz cries. "They're me! All those Mees out there! They're all ME!" he shrieks.

"Oh Chawz! I see me, I see me everywhere," Mara's heart is thumping!

"Oh no!" Chawz groans. "This is horrible." Then he yells out, "Help! Someone help!"

All of the Mees around them eerily play out their own scenes.

"The doors!" Mara gasps and pulls on Chawz. "Come on!"

More Mees appear. One Mara yells at a dog. Another curls against a column. One bumps Mara's shoulder, then disappears into the growing crowd. That Me by the well hugs an invisible person. That one says loving words. Another tears up her sketchbook—she tears up her sketchbook!

Mara and Chawz are able to make it to the very center of the room. But now they're directly underneath the chandelier.

Chawz screams. He grips onto Mara even tighter. Mara looks up, swaying back and forth.

The chandelier spreads out from its source.

Crumble. Crumble beneath it.

Mara whimpers, then laughs, then cries out. She clutches her arms to her front pocket.

The Mees suddenly stop. They turn. They fix their eyes on Mara and Chawz.

All at once their voices rise. "Terrible artist!" "Useless boy." "They don't like you." "I love you." "You're so talented!" "Stupid. Stupid." "You'll always be a loser." "You can't think of anything can you?" "Very impressive." "Auntie won't like you!"

Mara wraps her hands around her head. She tries to close her eyes, but they bolt back open. Chawz whimpers, "Why? Why? Why?"

Mara's about to bite through her lip. Chawz is about to tear his hair out.

But then suddenly, a light bursts into the room. Radiance sweeps between the Mees. They become silhouettes. Then they fade. Blessedly, like a miracle, they fade, fade away.

A person is standing there, holding the doors open.

Mara and Chawz both let out a sob. Chawz relaxes his grip on Mara's arm and hiccups.

The person walks quickly over to them, her long green robe swishes against the stone floor and her grey hair sparkles.

"Oh you poor things," she says. "Come here now." She

helps them stand, and Chawz and Mara instinctively grab onto the strange woman.

She holds them. "Don't worry, don't worry my dears, I turned off the strange effect of the chandelier. They're gone now. They're all gone."

After holding Mara and Chawz tightly for a moment, she says, "Come, I'll take you out of here."

Then the woman leads them away from the haunting light fixture and out of the cold, stone room.

Chapter 5: Practice

Still dazed by their experience in the horrible room filled with Mees, Mara and Chawz are guided by the strange, wonderful woman through sweet smelling caverns. Sunlight from far overhead dapples the walls. After not too long, she turns them through an archway into a grotto where several ponds ripple with the tickling of an underground stream.

Even in this place of lush, calm, beauty, Mara and Chawz still shiver and shake. Their eyes glance to the shadows, and little groans and gasps slip out with their stuttering breath. The woman sits them down on a mossy rise next to the largest pond.

"Some food will make you feel much better." She produces a tray with fruit, veggies and cheese. Chawz and Mara dive in.

"I'm Seergart," the woman says. "And I'm sorry that room scared you. It's supposed to be a consensual experience."

Chawz and Mara stuff their faces.

The grotto is so peaceful, the gentle tinkling of the stream plays like music. Soon the two eat their fill and their bodies calm a bit. But their minds still roil with a thousand yelling versions of themselves.

Seergart sweeps her hand and guides their gaze around the

room. "This grotto is a huge amplification chamber. Sounds flow in on the currents of the stream—the sounds of the stories of our world. These walls lift those quiet murmurs into clear song. And so I listen to Earth's orchestra."

Seergart kneels in the moss and tilts her head towards the water. "It's a kind of music. It's the music of Earth and her children. The tones of a thousand lifetimes."

She pulls a tuning fork from her robe and taps it on a rock. The fork sounds and Seergart waves it back and forth. "This tone is a D note. It's Earth's own tone."

She catches their eyes. "We each have our own tone. Can you hear yours? Can you sing yours? This stream has a tone, can you hear it?" Blue light shines through openings far overhead.

Mara and Chawz lock onto her words, trying to climb out the terror that still courses through their bodies and clouds their minds.

"I want to hear it," Mara says.

"Me too!" Chawz agrees.

Seergart beams at them, melting through a little more of their fear and disquiet. "Okay," she says. "This is the first song I ever truly heard. Lie back. That moss is comfortable isn't it? Now blur your listening. Even my voice becomes a part of the beautiful orchestra that plays for us. All sounds become one beautiful song. Let the gentle cadence of the nearby stream rise. Hear the sadness in its burbling and the circus in its sparkles. Hear it waltz with the stone, dancing, dancing, and hear it's tone!" She strikes two tuning forks together and their tones join seamlessly with the voice of the stream. Tears well through Mara's closed eyelids.

"A Minor." Seergart whispers. "Who you were, who you have become, who you will be—are all one. Or none."

Then she gently claps her hands. "The Quiet, we ask to join us." She chants, "Quiet in space and mind. We thank you."

And in the grotto, sound itself shies to the corners and alcoves.

Her voice barely disturbs the silence now. "In the room with the chandelier, the self fragments into thousands of discordant tones which vy for dominance. The room is called the I-solation chamber. The chandelier shows you visions of yourself, and allows you to face them. It's the path of the phoenix. Part of The Designer's fabulous creation."

"My Auntie!" Mara suddenly cries out as she remembers. She staggers to her feet and looks around. She remembers that there's something she's supposed to be doing. The voices in her head fade. "Auntie's creation?" Mara asks.

Seergart nods. "Easy now Mara. The Designer is your aunt? Yes, this house is her creation. She's one of the greatest artists in the world. But this house is a much bigger project than normal. A lot of really weird things happened. Accidentally I guess. Like the I-solation chamber for example."

"Greatest artist..." Mara says with wonder. Then she adds, "Yes, she's my aunt. And she needs my help."

Mara sucks in a quick breath and holds it. Then her face

melts into a big frown. "How am I gonna help though? The only thing I'm good at is drawing, and I might be really bad at that."

Seergart says, "I'll bet your aunt felt the same way about herself at one point Mara. Do you know she practices every day? Still! She'll sit and draw the same curve over and over and over again."

"That's one of her favorite words," Mara says.

"Which one?"

"Practice."

Seergart nods and winks at her.

The stream burbles. A breath of wind ripples the leaves of the vines and trees.

After a few false starts, Mara whispers, "I... I... I've never had an original idea."

Seergart nods slowly. "Mara, look at me," she says. Then she leans close. "I've never met anyone who's had an original idea."

"But what about Auntie?"

"Why don't you ask her about that when you see her, okay?"

Mara nods. "Okay."

"I think you'll be surprised by her answer. But you said she needed help?"

"Ya, I remember now. There's some invaders..." Mara hides one hand behind the other and points at Chawz.

"Ah, okay." Seergart reaches into her robes and then hands

Chawz several tuning forks. "Chawz, use these to find your very own sacred tone. Hum up and down until your body fully resonates." Chawz nods and starts practicing.

Seergart walks Mara to the door of the grotto. "Do you feel better?"

Mara nods. "I do. I feel a lot better, thank you. I just really want to find Auntie now."

"Where were you headed?"

"We were trying to get to Doctor Zhao's office."

"Oh that's nearby actually." Seergart points down the hallway. "Go all the way to the end, then head up the stairs. His office is at the first landing. And Mara, try to find your sacred tone. Hum up and down until you feel a powerful resonance. Your sacred tone can bring you calm when you need it most."

"Okay." Mara nods

"And keep practicing your drawing, you'll be a wonderful artist."

Mara glances at the ground, but then manages a little smile. "I hope so. Thank you, Seergart."

Chawz waves to Mara.

"Bye Chawz." She waves back.

He gives her two thumbs up. "I don't want to be an invader!"

That makes Mara giggle.

Seergart asks, "You're gonna be really cautious and go straight to Doctor Zhao's office and wait for him there, right?"

"I will."

"Good, he'll know what to do."

"Thank you Seergart." Mara says again.

Seergart winks.

Then Mara cautiously heads down the hallway towards Doctor Zhao's office, humming quietly up and down.

Chapter 6: Conflict

Mara feels so grateful to Seergart for rescuing her and
Chawz from the I-solation Room. She feels a lot better as she hums
her way down the hallway past large paintings, spirit washed with
trees and animals. She walks past hammered doors of bronze and
iron, others of plain wood, some earthy, some polished to shine.

None of this part of the house looks accidental to her.
Seergart's comment is haunting her a little, "bigger than normal...
weird things, accidental things happened." But Mara sees her
aunt's touch everywhere. Of course Auntie would choose wispy
paintings to go with old stone walls. On the other hand though,
Mara's never seen a trapdoor before, never anything like that in
one of Auntie's houses. Caverns, grottos, sure. Old stone chapels,
why not? But T-rexes? Hordes of wild primates? Invading armies?
No way. Mara decides that Auntie definitely needs her help.

She kicks it up to a run until she reaches the door at the end
of the hallway. She slips through the door, and then jumps up the
stairs, spiraling up, up, up. She runs onto the first landing and puts
her ear to the door. She doesn't hear anything so she cracks it open
and peeks inside.

She sees that she's at the back door to what must be Doctor

Zhao's office. She steps in and closes the door behind her. Through large windows to her left, sunlight brightens the dark wood interior. Just to her right, Doctor Zhao's desk looks towards the front door of the office. A few chairs face the desk, and more chairs accompany small tables in the corners. Lots of wooden filing cabinets and bookshelves hug the walls. And on every available surface, small models of machines, models of buildings, interiors, all sorts of models are set up. And each one is surrounded by an orderly grid of different colored sticky notes, which makes Mara grin.

The most unusual thing about Doctor Zhao's office is that there's a periscope which goes up through the ceiling. It looks just like what you'd see on a submarine. And even from all the way across the room, Mara can see that in its large viewing lens, an image of something shifts around.

Mara crosses past Doctor Zhao's desk to the periscope. She pushes a chair close and hops up onto it. Then she grabs the handles of the periscope and takes a look.

"Oh no!" she says as her eyebrows crinkle with concern.

In the viewing lens, she can see a rolling field between two hills. On one hill is a small army of people wearing leather and chainmail standing in a tight formation of lines. On the other hill is a swarming mass of shrieking, screaming people wearing antlers and horns on their helmets.

Just then, the door to the office suddenly swings open. Mara jumps, startled, and hits her head against the periscope.

"Ow!" she cries out and lurches. The chair she's standing on teeters over, but she throws her hands out, steps on the back of the chair as it goes down, and lands on her feet.

Doctor Zhao claps his hands from the doorway. "Very nice landing, Mara! Good to see you! I'm so glad you escaped."

Mara rubs her forehead with her eyes pressed closed.

"Oh no, are you ok? Here, let me get you some ice." Doctor Zhao crosses to a small fridge that blends in with the file cabinets.

"Oww," Mara whispers. Then she says aloud, "Doctor Zhao, the movie in this periscope looks really real."

"Oh yes, I should turn that off," Doctor Zhao answers. "That invention is quite a miracle I must say." He grabs some ice from the fridge, wraps it in a handkerchief and walks over and gives it to Mara.

Then he looks through the periscope. "It is currently showing Maewyn Succat conquering the last of the Druids."

"It looks so real though."

"The periscope, or Chronocular, as we call it, looks into the past. So what you're seeing is actually happening, but sixteen hundred years or so ago."

Mara blinks at him blankly.

So he continues, "Somehow this periscope is looking at Earth from the perspective of sixteen hundred or so light years away. And then zoomed in a lot. It's a big laser loop that goes out, way out into space, and allows us to watch the past."

"Wow," Mara says. "Umm… Can we use it to find

Auntie?"

"Hmm, maybe if we had a better idea of where to look. Why don't I get the map out." Doctor Zhao directs her to a chair opposite his desk and then heads over to a file cabinet. He opens it and flips through the files. "Your aunt has told me how capable you are."

"She has?"

"Oh yes, she talks about you a lot."

"Really? Wow. She's so amazing. I really want to show her my…" Mara stops.

Doctor Zhao glances up.

"Um… I was saying that I might show her my sketchbook."

"I'm sure she'd love to see your sketchbook." He says and then sticks his head all the way into the file cabinet. "Hmm not in this one." He switches to a set of drawers. "Mara, how did you escape?"

"I escaped... Oh, I fell into that horrible I-solation room with this boy Chawz, one of the bad guys. He's actually not so bad though. Then this really nice person, Seergart, saved us."

Doctor Zhou pulls out a really large folded up block of paper. "So the chandelier must have been left on. Hmm. Yes, Seergart is very nice. I'm glad you got to meet her." He uses his hip to push closed the drawer, then heads back over to his desk. "I've only heard about the I-solation room, I've not had a chance to try it myself. I hear it's a very intense, personal experience."

"Yes." Mara nods.

"I'll have to try it at some point. But, you'll see, this house is quite large and I haven't visited that much of it yet."

Mara stands up on her chair to see better. "That's the map?"

"It's the best we have." He pushes the jars of pencils and the abacus and all the other items on his desk out of the way. "But this isn't perfect. It's actually just copies of all of your aunt's drawings all taped together the best we can figure out. Mara, just to let you know, your aunt might have bitten off a little more than she could chew with this house. There are lots of rooms, like the I-solation room, that are a little strange, or very strange even."

Mara's eyebrows are getting pretty sore from being amazed all the time. She's just gonna have to roll with this.

Doctor Zhao laughs a little uncomfortably. "I'm sure it will turn out fine. We're still exploring it all to be honest. But I think... I think I might know what the invaders are after."

Doctor Zhao tries to unfold the piecemeal map, but sections start refolding. Kinks crumple the corners. "Stop this you..." he says. An edge of the map whips up and baps him in the head. "Hey!" He pushes it back down, but new kinks form and unfolded sections start thomping across the desk. Mara reaches out several times, but has to leap back as the map flaps and slaps.

"To the floor with you!" Doctor Zhao suddenly shouts. Mara jumps out of the way as Doctor Zhao swoops around the desk with the contorted map folded over his head. He dives and body slams it to the floor. Using all fours, he kicks and punches and kicks until the rowdy map finally settles down.

"Now then." Doctor Zhao gets back up and smooths his suit with some gentle swipes of his hand.

The map is really really big. It fills the open space on the floor. It's made of hundreds of pages of Auntie's drawings that are all taped together. The map itself is a sprawling, surreal expression of the house. Mara is blown away by how many buildings there are. And there's towers and domes and caverns also. The scattered grouping of structures is all surrounded by thick woods and wilds.

"Auntie drew all these," Mara says with wonder.

"Yes, yes she did."

Mara slowly walks around it. "There's so much."

"Maybe a bit too much, to be honest," Doctor Zhao says.

"But Doctor Zhao, how did Auntie accidentally build things? How did weird, strange things happen? None of this makes any sense."

"I know. It doesn't." Doctor Zhao nods. "Mara, are you able to save that question for Auntie? The answer is hers to share, her secret, not mine."

"I guess so." Mara nods.

Mara thinks that Auntie's drawings, all taped together, sort of do make a good map. Different groups of drawings form the sections, and there's lots of close ups of rooms, and lots of notes.

"Everything is so detailed," she whispers. She feels that glow she gets when she looks at Auntie's drawing. The edges of her mouth curl up into a big grin. She can see the confidence in Auntie's lines.

In the center is a group of drawings that show a large overview of the house with all of its buildings and surrounding wilderness. Around the perimeter is that little black rock wall Mara first climbed over by the gaudy cars. The wall in Auntie's drawing sparkles just like the real one. The narrow moat is there too, with the blobs. It goes all the way around too. It's barely visible—Mara has to lean close to see it. And there's the Rex Brothers also, in the woods! They're hanging out with that gang of primates.

Mara almost can't believe how wonderful the map is. She takes a step back. She thinks Auntie is the most amazing artist. Mara's own drawings feel rough and wild in comparison. She wonders if she'll ever be a great artist. Maybe the greatest title she'll ever achieve is Miss. Scribbles. She doesn't even realize how bad she's frowning.

But Doctor Zhao notices. "Mara, are you okay? Is your head badly hurt?" he asks.

She shakes her head. "No I'm okay, I'm okay."

"All right, you let me know." He twinkles his fingers at her and smiles.

She sorta smiles back, then she sets the ice pack down on his desk and feels her forehead. "I'm fine."

But then Mara notices a small totally blank spot on the map. "What's that?" She points at it.

"Wow," Doctor Zhao says. "Okay, I guess I shouldn't be

surprised that that's your first question, but let's not jump to the end so quick." He grabs a laser pointer from his pen jar. "So this is The House of the Human, as your aunt has named it."

"The House of the Human?"

"Yes, The Designer felt most inspired by this name."

The map shows that The House of the Human spreads through the mountain range. Wild woods encircle a vast collection of buildings. Towers stand in the tall trees. Domes huddle alongside giant boulders. And under the surface, a massive network of caverns and tunnels are shown through windows of subtle shading and color.

All the shapes of the buildings and the grounds seem to create a larger image to Mara. "Is it a baby?" she asks.

"Ha!" Doctor Zhao claps. "Of course you would see it so quickly. Although your Aunt had no babies of her own, she's had many children, and this is one of them. A wild one though. Look here."

Doctor Zhao uses his pointer to underline a scrawling title that stretches like a spider's web towards the center of the map. It reads, *Past and Present*. "Pretty much the entire house is in the 'Past and Present.' But then there's that small blank spot you pointed out. Go ahead, you can walk on the map. Get real close and read what the blank spot says."

Mara takes a few steps onto the map and bends close. Then she gets all the way down onto her hands and knees.

There's two super tiny words there.

She puts her head almost down to map. "*The Future*," Mara reads, then she sits up on her knees. "What's in 'The Future'?"

"No clue," Doctor Zhao says.

"Uhh..." Mara rubs her forehead.

"Well, generally, we know that there's a large vault there. But we don't know what's in the vault.'"

"Is that what the bad guys want?" Mara says. "We need to find Auntie."

"Yes we do." Doctor Zhao circles *The Future* with his laser. "And yes, I do think that the invaders are after whatever is inside the vault. But I really doubt they'll have any chance of getting it open. So I think their first priority will be to capture your aunt."

Seeing Mara's frown, he quickly adds, "Hopefully the invaders just get lost and go home."

"I don't want them to capture her," Mara says.

"Me neither." Doctor Zhao points to a subterranean city called Undercanyon. "Your aunt had a meeting this morning in Undercanyon. I did try calling a number of her offices, but no luck." He circles a small cursive *A* on the map near Undercanyon. "This is one of her offices. We could try to meet up with her there. Although I do wish we could find out who the invaders are." He taps his foot.

"What about the Chronoculator?" Mara asks. "Can't we look back just a few hours into the garden?"

"That's a really good idea Mara! The Chronocular." He

tosses his laser pointer back into the penholder and crosses to the Chronocular. Looking into the viewing lens, he adjusts the dials on both sides.

Mara pulls up a chair next to him and stands on it.

Doctor Zhao backs his head up a bit. "Yes, here, we can both look." He keeps fussing with the dials.

Contorted imagery twists around the screen of the Chronocular as he pans through time and space. "Okay good," he says as he lands the image on the gardens of The House of the Human. Then he zooms way in.

Mara can see that the gardens were truly beautiful and lush before the river raged through. In the Chronocular, the river is still small and gentle. It weaves under several delicate bridges, and then branches into streams that fill a scattering of pools. Flowering bushes and fruiting trees splash color into the abundance of green growth. She can see Sarah's little house. It's a little one room hut with a thatched roof right near the river bank.

"Sarah's house is cute," Mara says.

But as they watch, the first wave of invaders slams through the doors in the huge rock wall. The soldiers spread out and then sweep towards the house. More soldiers stream through. Then the group with the glittering accessories saunters in.

"I think those are the leaders." Mara points at them.

Doctor Zhao zooms in, then says, "Oh. Yes. Oh my, the woman there—I know her." He points at a steel eyed woman in a long, feathered, dark-blue coat. "Oh my." Doctor Zhao frowns.

"Who is she?" Mara asks as she checks the snap on her front pocket.

"That is the greedy Lady Banks." Doctor Zhao shakes his head. "The rest must be very powerful, very powerful indeed to be so casual around her. My my."

Doctor Zhao, looking very concerned, switches off the Chronocular. "We must find your Aunt before she does. And I think our best bet once we find your aunt is to temporarily evacuate the house."

"Evacuate the house? But what if that Banks lady goes into The Future and opens the vault?"

"She'll never be able to open the vault, the key is…"

But then the phone rings.

They both jump at the noise and Doctor Zhao actually grimaces at the phone. It rings again and its red light blinks insistently.

Mara whispers, "Do you want me to answer it? Maybe it's Auntie."

Doctor Zhao sighs. "No, she doesn't call on that line." He sits down at his desk, then picks up the phone and holds it between them so Mara can hear, but he also puts his finger over his mouth. Mara nods to him. Then Doctor Zhao says into the phone, "Hello?..."

Out of the phone flows a beautiful voice with just a rasp of age, "Doctor Zhao you're there, thank goodness." Auntie! Mara almost shouts out, but Doctor Zhao sternly motions for her to remain silent. Mara can feel his fear. Her brow furrows and her eyes cloud.

"Yes!" Doctor Zhao responds. "Are you okay my dear Designer?"

Auntie doesn't answer though.

"She's fine," another woman's sharp edged voice slices through the phone line.

"Oh no," Mara whispers.

Doctor Zhao puts his finger over his mouth again and shakes his head at Mara. She nods. She feels like bursting into tears.

"The Lady Banks," Doctor Zhou answers.

"Yes, Doctor Zhou." The greedy Lady Banks laughs a cold-hearted mocking laugh. "I'm surprised to say we've already captured your great Designer. She walked right into our arms, imagine that. But now she says she doesn't know where the key is."

"May I speak with her please?" Doctor Zhou hunches his shoulders.

"I WANT THE KEY!"

Doctor Zhao and Mara jump back and cringe. Then Doctor Zhao replies, "Ah...what key..."

"THE KEY! You know which key!"

"No, I..."

"THE KEY!"

"Ahhh! Aii!"

"DOCTOR ZHAO!" Then in a hiss, "Your Designer is taking me to the room called The Future. You better be there waiting for us with the vault key."

"Ohh! No! But I don't know where the key is!"

"FIND IT! And if I were you, I'd steer clear of my minions. This silly house is interfering with our communications. I'd hate to have them waste your precious time by capturing you."

"But I don't know where the key is!"

Click.

"Oh my." Doctor Zhao slowly sets down the phone. "She doesn't seem very nice."

"Not at all." Mara shakes her head. "You really don't know where the key is?"

"I don't even know *what* the key is," Doctor Zhao says.

"What do you mean?"

"Well, ever since your aunt built the house, the vault door has been closed. On the door is a circular impression, like the size of a ping pong ball, which is the keyhole, so to speak. But that's it, there's no handle or number pad. The only other thing we know is that the key is broken into different pieces, and the pieces are hidden throughout the house."

"Auntie doesn't know where they are?"

"No she doesn't"

"Who does?"

"No one does," Doctor Zhao says.

"That's kinda weird Doctor Zhao."

"Yes. There are many weird things about this house." He nods.

Mara rubs her forehead. "Well, do we try to rescue Auntie? Or do we look for the key?"

Doctor Zhou shakes his head. "There's no way we can overpower The Lady Banks and her army. She's extremely well funded. But there is one thing that has me wondering though. Auntie could have avoided them. She could have disappeared into the house and they would have never found her. Personally, I think she wanted to be captured."

"Really?"

"I do, I think so, but I don't have any clue why she would let herself be captured." Doctor Zhao gets up and looks back at the map for a moment. Then he shakes his head and says, "So, with that in mind, I say we try to find the key and trade it for Auntie. Better to play along with The Lady Bank's game until we know more."

"Should we be worried about her getting whatever is in the vault."

"To be honest, we don't even know if there's anything in there. It could be empty for all we know. Auntie is more important."

"Yes. Auntie is more important." Mara nods. "So we've got to find that key then."

"Yes we do. Unfortunately Mara, I'm not so sure where we should start looking. The house is absolutely huge."

Mara leans over the edge of the map. "It's super huge."

"Go ahead, walk on it, maybe you'll get an idea."

Mara takes a few gentle steps back onto the map. After a moment of wandering, she kneels down and explores on her hands and knees. Doctor Zhao moves around the edge, frowning and shaking his head from time to time.

Mara leans into a group of surface buildings. "This one building says 'The Otherworld Artist's Community, but it looks like a big warehouse."

"Dancers, acrobats, musicians. Keep looking."

Mara crawls over several mountain peaks. "Here's a lonely valley called 'Party Kingdom'?"

"I don't know about that." Doctor Zhao takes a deep breath. "I just don't know Mara."

Mara moves her lips back and forth, then points at an enormous subterranean room. "Is that an ocean?"

"Believe it or not, yes. Somehow that happened." Doctor Zhao says.

Mara looks close at a tiny island in the middle of the underground ocean. "Oracle," she says and then sits up sharply. "Auntie says, when you're lost, find an Oracle."

"She does, does she?"

Mara nods.

He looks at her intensely for a moment. "You know what Mara?"

"What?"

"You might be the only person who can find this key."

She scrunches her face. "Why do you say that?"

"Because you know your aunt better than anyone."

Mara's eyebrows go up, she moves her hand up to her sketchbook.

Chapter 7: Renaissance

After their shocking call with the greedy Lady Banks, and Mara's insightful idea to seek out the Oracle, Doctor Zhao leads Mara through a series of fairly normal business-type corridors. She can hear the buzz of office bees behind the closed doors to either side. Their journey eventually takes them to an area of the house that seems very old to Mara with dark wooden walls and small cloudy windows. At the end of the long corridor, he pushes through some heavy doors into the room with the giant ocean.

"Wow," Mara says.

"It's crazy right?." Doctor Zhao stands next to her and shields his brow. Salty mist sprays across their faces. Waves splash against the jagged rocks they stand on, and whitecaps extend into the horizon.

"It really is an ocean," Mara says.

"Yup." Doctor Zhao nods.

Before them, a small calm bay opens up to deep and wild ocean waters that stretch into the horizon. Behind them are the heavy wooden sea doors they entered through. The wall the doors are in, curves around the little bay and climbs in a slow arch until the wood merges into the sky.

Mara points up. "That's real sky?"

"Sort of," Doctor Zhou says. "The ceiling extends all the way over the ocean, but it has holes in it, like swiss cheese, to let in the sun and the rain and what not, the birds."

"Wow."

"Your aunt created quite the wonder here."

"I don't think I'll ever be as good an artist as her." Mara drops the rock she was gonna throw into the waves.

"Everything takes time and practice Mara. You already have the key ingredient."

"What's that?"

"You love to draw."

The ocean turns deep blue a ways out. Mara's got a couple of sketchbooks with underwater creatures. One of them is full of whales. "I do love to draw," she says.

Doctor Zhao nods, then pulls out a compass and checks their direction. "You ready to go to the Oracle?"

"Ya, but how are we gonna get there?" Mara says.

"Come on." Doctor Zhao leads her back across the rocks to the doors and they head through. "We're going to build a boat," he says.

"Really?" Mara's never built a boat.

"You'll see, I'm hoping we get a little help."

In the moist wooden hallway, the daylight seeps in through foggy window panes.

"Why isn't there anyone around here?" Mara asks.

"Actually, lots of parts of the house aren't inhabited yet. But there are a few people who work down here already, just not all the time."

Doctor Zhao stops at a set of doors in the left wall and reaches into his pocket. "Wait, those varmints took my keys!" He slaps his jacket, then his pants. "Oh no, oh no."

Mara reaches past him and tries the knob. "It's open Doctor Zhao."

"Oh thank goodness!" he exclaims and pushes into the room.

Inside, heavy rows of shelving, stacked with five gallon plastic water bottles, stretch beyond the meager light cast by the two dim bulbs that hang from the beams overhead. The light doesn't even reach up through the beams, so there's no sense of the ceiling at all.

Doctor Zhao walks a little ways into the rows, then turns back and says, "Hrrm...Well, let's get a cart. You load up empty bottles, and I'll grab some full ones." He rolls out one of the three heavy carts that are parked in the front of the room.

"Water bottles?" Mara asks.

"We'll build a boat out of them."

"Like a raft?"

"I'm thinking something nicer than that, but basically, we're gonna tie them together and make a boat."

"Oh." Mara puffs her mouth full of air. "Okay."

But then, Doctor Zhao suddenly spins towards the back of

the room.

Mara edges behind the cart. "Is something there?" she whispers.

A high pitched voice screams from the back of the room, "Yes there is!" Then much closer, the same voice, "If you take from us, you'll be sore."

"Doctor Zhao?" Mara crouches lower.

Doctor Zhou yells, "Tepe! It's Doctor Zhao. We need your help."

But he gets drowned out by the scary voice that's now directly above them, "High Security! High Security!"

"Doctor Zhao!" Mara rushes over to him and grabs his coat.

But Doctor Zhao stomps his foot. "Tepe! Stop this right now!" Then, in a more gentle voice, "Tepe, please come down here. I know these bad people in the house have upset you. I know."

After a moment, a small head bobs down out of the shadows above them with a little frown. Then a slender arm drops, followed by a torso and two legs, and the tiny little man hangs there from his other arm, swinging gently. He points at Mara. "What's your name?"

Mara lets go of Doctor Zhao. "I'm Mara," she says quietly.

Then Tepe just lets go of the beam and falls.

"Oh no!" Mara gasps.

But the little man sails down, hits the floor on all fours, and just as his body compresses to the ground, he springs back into a bounce more than twice his height, and then lands gently on his feet.

Mara claps for him. "That was neat."

Tepe scratches under his chin.

Doctor Zhao introduces them, "Mara, Tepe. Tepe, Mara. Mara's The Designer's niece."

"Oh ya?" Tepe says. He's just a little shorter than Mara and looks really cool. Leather garb flows in a web around his sinewy muscles. His gloves don't cover his fingers, and his sandals look like part of his feet. Straps around his arms and legs hold small pouches, and he has dark flaring eyebrows.

"We have to save Auntie," Mara says.

"The bad people got her?" Tepe asks.

"Ya, the bad people, they captured her." Doctor Zhao nods.

"What do they want?"

"They want to get into the vault, and they're forcing us to find the key."

"Where's the key?"

"It's hidden somewhere in the house."

"Will you help us find it?" Mara asks.

Tepe snorts. "Well of course."

So the three of them get to work. For the next little bit, Mara and Doctor Zhao load full water bottles and cart them out to the rocks, while Tepe works on the empties with a large spool of twine.

After Mara and Doctor Zhao's sixth cart-load, a nice big pile of full water bottles is stacked near the edge of the water.

But then a loud bonging and blanging from the hallway booms over the crash of the nearby waves. Doctor Zhao and Mara move towards the doors, but after a few steps they stop and start backing up.

Countless bangs on top of bongs on top of clangs.

Doctor Zhao and Mara cover their ears and scramble behind two boulders.

Tepe bursts through the door, jumping in large springs and soaring through the air, then bouncing off the ground again. He pulls a massive snake of empty five gallon water bottles that hoots and hollers in its blangy bong language.

Tepe halts and snaps the line. His bottle-snake whips cleanly into a coil.

"What are you guys doing?" he asks.

Doctor Zhao stands back up, then shouts at Tepe, "SO LOUD!"

Tepe looks blank for a moment, then pulls a swab of leather from each ear. "What?" he asks.

Doctor Zhao rubs his brow and shakes his head.

The three begin tying together water bottles to build the boat. Doctor Zhou gives instructions and places bottles in position, while Tepe scurries around using his hands and feet to tie everything together. Mara hustles bottles over to them, and also helps Tepe with the twine when he calls for help. After a ton of work, they step back, catch their breath and take a look at the boat they've built.

"It's so cool," Mara says. "You're really good at building things Doctor Zhao."

"Why thank you," he nods. "This boat is a twenty foot sloop with a mainsheet and a jib."

They hop over the row of bottles which form the railing, and stand on the deck. Doctor Zhou checks the knotting around the boat. He runs his hand over the bottles, touching here, tugging there, all the way up the sweeping deck to the pointed bow. He whistles over the waves, puts his finger into the air, then walks back down and shakes the mast. It wobbles a little, but the bottles are tied tight. He signals up to the crows nest and Tepe scrambles up the mast and takes his position there. Doctor Zhao winks at Mara. "You know what to do?"

Mara nods. "I'll work the sails with the lines like how you told me."

"You'll do great, it's gonna be a smooth ride." Doctor Zhao undoes the mooring rope and takes hold of the rudder, then he shouts out, "Unfurl the sails!"

Mara loosens the knots holding the jib and mainsheet in place, and then runs over to the pulleys and grabs her lines. The two big tarps flutter limply for a moment, but then Mara pulls a bit and the sails pop full of wind.

"Here we go!" Doctor Zhao yells.

The boat skims swiftly over the gentle waves. The light

salty mist cools them, and the water bottles reflect the sun into thousands of sparkles that dance with the boat's motion. Soon, the rocks are forgotten behind them and the waves stretch into the distance.

After some time, sailing across the ocean, Mara hollers back to Doctor Zhao, "I thought we'd see the other side of the room by now."

"It's a massive room Mara."

"Is there really a ceiling?"

"There sure is."

"It's hard to tell," she says.

In the blue water, large schools of fish and turtles take their time, swimming lazily around. And then, whales come to swim alongside them. "Whales!" Mara yells. "Auntie loves whales! She says they're full of love and curiosity."

After a wonderful visit, the whales head off on their own way, and as the trio sails onwards, Mara, in her mind, draws a whole nother sketchbook full of deep sea creatures.

Suddenly, she jolts back to reality when Tepe shouts, "Island!"

Doctor Zhao shifts the boat in the direction Tepe is pointing and soon enough, an island rises over the horizon.

The tiny turtle-back of land is overgrown by an olive grove and curling grape vines. There's an old, classic looking marble building right in the center of the little island with columns and a sacred air that makes Mara think of old temples and sacred shrines.

The trees and vines encompass the structure, clothing the marble building and its tall columns in green.

A short stone pier juts out from the island, and while Tepe and Mara furl the sails, Doctor Zhao coasts them up to the pier. When they get close enough to dock, Tepe hops off and ties the mooring lines tight.

Doctor Zhao leads them off the boat and up the short incline to the building. They stop at the foot of the steps leading up to the front doors.

"It looks so old," Mara says.

"Apparently, this isn't its original location, but it has always been the home of the Oracle," Doctor Zhao says. He walks up and knocks on the doors. The sound echoes and the rustling of the trees quiets as the wind stills.

Then, from atop the building, a girl's light voice calls down, "Why do you come here?"

Mara and her friends back down the stairs to look up at her. The girl has pushed grape leaves to the side, and is leaning over the edge of a short wall which runs around the roof of the building.

"We hope to see the Oracle please," Doctor Zhao calls up.

The girl looks them over for a moment, then says, "The Oracle's clarity is a mystery. How will you be able to hear her?"

Doctor Zhao, with an oath-like response says, "We'll strive to understand with our minds, to feel with our hearts, and to join with our spirits."

Mara looks up at him. For some reason, he sounded like a

spinning triangle to her.

After a lapse where the waves lap and a seagull's call pierces the sky, the girl says, "Stay there."

She reappears a few minutes later from around the side of the building. The girl is wearing a green dress tied with soft slender vines that flows around her like the breeze. A braided hoop holds back her hair, and she steps lightly on the moss and stones with her bare feet. Mara thinks she's beautiful.

"The Oracle will speak to you," the girl says. "Please follow me." She leads them onto a big gathering of vines that climbs up the side of the building. They walk up the vines to the roof where a garden of broad-leaved plants flower and dip beneath small trees. Off to their left, near the front of the building, the plants grow wild and dense, but to their right, towards the back of the building, there's an open area with a mirror-still pool of water. Beyond the pool is a copse of trees. And the branches of these trees have been woven into a thick canopy which shelters a small room. Light shines from within, and a woman is standing silhouetted in its entrance.

The Oracle.

She glides out of her home to the small pool and motions for the group to join her around the still waters. They approach. The Oracle's voice is calm and filled with the depth of one that is long-lived and well-experienced. She says, "Listen and allow me to guide your respect." Her eyes trace the world around her in slow curves and they flare again and again, but land nowhere.

After several minutes pass, she speaks in a solemn voice, "Two curious ones came with questions about the ancients. I sent them to the ruins. They revived lost knowledge, but this knowledge was used to build empires."

"We won't do that," Mara whispers.

The Oracle nods, "I feel the truth in your words." Then she leans over the pool. Impossibly, her body stretches and grows and bends into a huge arch. She peers directly down into the mirror pond. Her fingers trace the waters in spirals and stars and moons.

"Slaves and riches, curious only about gold. Plagues and poxes, the exchange of life." The Oracle and her reflection writhe. Then she cries out, "Globe Island is vulnerable! Cleanse yourselves in the salty waters!"

Reaching into her robe, The Oracle hands each of them a small vial filled with some sort of cloudy green gas. "Fill your bodies full, breathe this deeply. But wait until the open waters have swallowed you."

Then The Oracle rises and with a wild reclamation of her arms, she bears her full focus upon Doctor Zhao and Tepe and Mara.

"Passion without partner. Hunter without home. Talent without teacher." Her voice speaks in wind, fire, earth and water, and her voice is unified by love.

"Find the heart, find the mind, and allow that which is eternal to flow free."

Then she bends towards the pool again. Her face lowers,

her arms splay up and behind, her fingers curl, and her hair blows wildly, as if fierce wind rises from the still water. The Oracle's neck stretches down and she submerges her face. Suddenly, shockingly, her feet lift into the sky. She flutters and whips around, her face held tight by the still pool.

Mara, Doctor Zhou, and Tepe, they step back in awe.

Then the Oracle pops up, pulling a fountain of water with her. She whips through the air like a rapidly deflating balloon, but then she lands gently in front of them.

"Health embraces disease, choice liberates thought." Her fingers brush the air as she turns away. "Spin the heart with your heart, draw that which our history has misplaced, and the doors will open. But be warned, you welcome within, those who would tear the world apart. The archway, the seventh sense. All things will end and begin with an embrace."

The oracle turns then, and recedes into her shadowy copse and is gone.

For a few moments Mara and her friends just stand there. Then Mara pinches herself. "Am I dreaming?" she says aloud.

Doctor Zhao reaches into his coat, pulls out a handkerchief and wipes his eyes, then he looks down at her. "Sometimes I wonder that myself," he says. "The world is filled with mystery."

"It sure is," Mara nods. After a moment she asks, "Where do we go now, Doctor Zhao?"

"Globe Island is the only place she mentioned."

"She said Globe Island is weeping. How can an island

cry?"

"I'm not sure. But I suppose we'll find out. Shall we then? Tepe?"

Mara and Tepe both nod.

"Okay," Doctor Zhao says. He and Tepe start heading back to the ramp, but Mara looks back at the Oracle's home. Her home is really all woven from living trees. Just like the plant spaceship in Mara's sketchbook. And there's tiny little flowers woven through it. Mara takes a few steps closer.

"Mara?" Doctor Zhao calls to her.

"Oh right," she says, then with a last glance she turns and runs to catch up.

The three make their way down off the roof. They gather on the pier next to their water bottle boat. It's mast wobbles with the waves.

Chapter 8: Exploration

The ocean is vast, and the sky is deep and blue. Mara, Doctor Zhao and Tepe sail away from the island of the Oracle. A steady wind blows and their boat swifts through the gentle waves. Mara ties the sail lines tight and goes to hang out at the back of the boat with Doctor Zhou.

"So how big is Globe Island? And why do think the Oracle said that it's weeping?" she asks. The thought of a whole island weeping makes her feel sad.

Doctor Zhou checks his compass and shifts the rudder to the right slightly. "Globe Island isn't that small, but it's a no-go zone in the house. The people on the island are supposed to be left alone," he says. "Technically we're breaking the rules by going there, but I don't know what else to do. We'll see. A lot of what the Oracle said just doesn't make any sense to me yet."

Mara agrees. "She sounded like a weird poem. She was so intense—I'm going to draw her. I'm gonna do an Oracle sketchbook full of prophecies. I think Auntie would like that."

"I'm sure she would," Doctor Zhou nods.

"I want to..." Mara bites her lip and presses her eyes closed.

Doctor Zhao pats her on the back. "We're gonna save your

aunt Mara," he says.

She rubs her eyes with her sleeves, then bites her lip harder. She wasn't thinking about Auntie. She was thinking that her oracle sketchbook will probably just be a bunch of silly scribbles. She wasn't even thinking about... Mara looks out at the waves and sniffs.

"Ya," she finally says.

After a few minutes, she asks, "What do you think these little vials the Oracle gave us do?"

But just then, Tepe, who's standing up on the very tip of the crow's nest, holding on with only his toes, yells down, "Two things are coming this way!" He points back behind them with both his hands.

"What do you see?" Doctor Zhao shouts up.

"It looks like two huge birds. Really big though!"

Mara and Doctor Zhao watch them rise over the horizon. And it does look like two huge birds gliding low and fast, straight towards them.

"There's something on the surface below them!" Tepe shouts. "Two people are surfing behind the birds!"

Doctor Zhao yells up to him, "They're not birds! They're Kites! Kite-surfers!"

"Yes! Yes! Kites!" Tepe shouts.

Doctor Zhao, with a new intensity, says, "Mara, get to the sails. Find as much wind as you can. We've got to lose them."

Mara rushes back over to the lines. Her heart is thumping

now. Somehow the whole idea of bad guys hadn't really clicked for her, but now it hits home like a load of bricks. Her face contorts desperately between fear and anger. She grabs the lines and tries to get as much wind into the sails as she can find. Her hands are shaking and her eyes are getting teary, but she can feel the boat jumping forward with her efforts.

The two kite-surfers are fast though. They're catching up quickly. Glancing over her shoulder, Mara can see that they're dressed all in black. Seemingly identical, their sharp boards scream off the waves, launching high and soaring through the air before they slice back into the water.

"They're gaining fast!" Tepe hollers.

"If only there were some rain to batter those kites," Doctor Zhao says. "Mara try to get more speed!"

"They're full!" she yells. These guys with the kites look so mean. Mara wants to scream, but instead she growls her feelings away and ties off the lines.

"Go away!" Tepe yells at the invaders. "Go away!"

The surfers race up to them. They split apart, and sweep to each side of the ship.

From their right, one of them yells, "Furl your sails!"

From their left, the other yells, "Prepare to be boarded!"

"Mara what are you doing?" Doctor Zhao hollers.

Mara's drawing in her sketchbook. Her hair whips around her and her pencil flies across the page. Shapes form and shadows loom, she slashes at the page, scattering diagonal streaks. She draws furiously, intensely, forgetting everything around her, until she darkens one last fatal curve. Then she spins her pencil around and pushes her hair out of her face.

Please work.

Her drawing flickers, then it flares brilliant purple. *Yes!* Light dances from her lines and cascades into the air in purple streams, sparkle and bright. The light pulls at her drawing and her shapes glow and stretch into the air. It's so bright—Mara shields her eyes. She did it, she did it!

Tepe shouts with a new type of horror. He shouts at the top of his lungs, "STOOOORM!"

The churning wall of storm that has suddenly appeared in front of them reaches to the sky. They crash right into it at full speed.

And so do the Kite surfers. The surfer to the left is immediately yanked out of the water. Fierce winds pull him up, up, over the boat, and he's flipped away.

"Oh no," Mara whispers. The storm is much bigger than she intended. Trying not to fall out of the bucking boat, she quickly stuffs her sketchbook into her pocket and snaps it closed.

"Furl the sails!" Doctor Zhao screams.

Mara frees the lines and the sails flap wildly.

The boat flounders and churns. The waves are getting higher and higher, and rain lashes down upon them.

The surfer to their right pulls on his kite, but the rain pounds it till it droops and sags. His board begins to sink as he loses speed.

Tepe slips down the mast to help Mara. They heave and pull at the tarps until they get both sails fully wrapped.

As they finish, a swiping wind curls down and grabs the remaining surfer's kite and flings him up into the clouds.

Mara gulps and frowns. She hopes the surfers are gonna be okay.

Just then, the boat lurches as a wave slams against it. The wave splashes over the rail and pounds down onto Mara. It tears her from the railing and takes her sliding across the deck. Arms flailing, she flops towards the mast and just barely catches ahold of it. Pulling herself close, struggling against the rushing water, Mara wraps herself tightly around the mast.

Then the storm completely consumes them. Wind thrown waves of ocean and rain smash over their heads. Larger, larger, and the wind screams louder and louder until huge folds of salty blue crash down and submerge them. The water bottle boat pops back up from the depths, high into the air. For the three poor humans in the boat, it takes all they have not to get thrown off. As their boat shoots up into the air, their feet fly up off the deck, and for a moment, they float suspended, and then they crash down to the deck again as the boat splashes back into the ocean.

The storm thickens and their beating worsens as the waves churn to deafening heights. Thunder echoes their crashing from on high. They're getting pummelled into blobs of flailing flesh, each round of submersion and expulsion more and more intense. In their time above the surface, the storm's vast whispers of sleep and weep urge them to let go, to give in. And under the water, each time a little longer, the cool echo of the ocean's conspiratorial agreement sucks at their will with promises of a deep dark and cold place to sleep forever and to never feel pain again.

It's in the stillness at the very depth of their plunges, and then again at the summit of their flights, that they get a brief moment to see each other. Doctor Zhao is wedged against the short back wall of the ship and he tries to control the rudder with one arm, clinging to the railing with the other. Mara is clutching the mast, and she spins around it as the waves lash and the boat lurches. Tepe is locked onto the center of the deck with his hands and feet and he rides the storm. Tepe's eyes gleam with focus, but Mara's grip weakens, and Doctor Zhao crashes and yelps.

The boat slides fast down the slick backside of a wave into a deep trough between swells. The whistle of the wind rises to a shriek and if it's possible, Doctor Zhao's face falls even deeper. Mara shudders at the feeling she gets from him, and she glances over her shoulder.

In front of them, the clouds themselves caress the peak of the mountainous wave that is still gathering its forces. The wave rises higher and higher. The water bottle boat races toward it. Dragged in by the wave's slippery tongue, their boat passes through the bottom of the trough. Above them, the crest of the wave peeks back down through the black clouds and leers at them. Sucked in by its unstoppable currents, they flow up the stomach of the wave. Faster and faster, until they rush straight up, up, up, until they crash through clouds and begin to curl over backwards.

With an upside down splash, they fall away from the precipice of water and tumble down into the chaos of the wave's vast tube. The boat spins wildly in the churn of air and then it slams right into the massive plunging wavecrest. The foamy tumult crushes them. It tears them like a flea from the sky and they plummet, with a whole sea of water following them down to the ocean far below.

Mara, Tepe, and Doctor Zhao fight to breathe. Falling through the air, they're mostly submerged in the wave, a strange downward floating. Then the wave's momentum rips a hole in itself and they're airborne again, flailing in a bubble encompassed by millions of gallons of water.

Fish fly with them. The fish try to swim in the tirade, but flip uselessly in the bubbles. They gasp in the air with the same panicked eyes that Mara has while struggling to hold her breath while underwater. She thinks the fish probably have a better chance in the long run.

World awash, all is a blur and the humans sense, more than see, the terrifying rapid approach of the ocean below.

Then…

Impact!

A mirror crashing into shards, swallowed by an angry whirlpool of loathsome cold chaos. They're pushed deep under water. All three of them are ripped away from the boat. Mara holds her breath and clutches her sketchbook. Deeper and deeper the wave pushes her down. She presses her eyes closed, tossed around in the abyssal frenzy of churning water and bubbling madness. The storm will be her last drawing! And it doesn't matter that her purple magic worked because she's never gonna get to draw again. She wishes she could somehow apologize to Auntie. She grasps at the snap on her front pocket.

Suddenly, a cold hand grabs her ankle. She tries to kick free, but the grip is iron. She looks down. It's Tepe! And he's got Doctor Zhou also. He pulls the three of them close together, and they form a ring, holding hands, and they stare into each other's eyes as they spin deeper and deeper. Tears from Mara's eyes join the salty ocean water. She realizes that Tepe hasn't saved them— Tepe's brought them together to die together.

Mara's heart sinks deeper than ever before. Her lungs are about to burst. She grabs at her chest. She's about to give in and breath the salty water. But just then, she feels the Oracle's vial in her pocket! She rips out the little vial.

Tepe and Doctor Zhao immediately do the same. To earn a few more seconds of life the three rip the stoppers out with their teeth, and they breathe in the vapor.

The little vial fills their lungs full with the green gas.

In a heartbeat, mystic communion: dissolution of the self— long slow stirring and an awakening of ages. The sanctuary of home, the endless embrace of mother and father, the boundless curiosity of son and daughter—The House of the Human.

In that cosmic moment, Auntie's house evolves into the body for a powerful beneficent spirit. And with a low sound, this Spirit of the House of the Human calls forth saviours from deep in the ocean.

A tingling runs through Mara, through Tepe, through Doctor Zhao, through their entire beings. A thousand thoughts and images. Insects flow over and under trees. Trees hold nests for birds who fly in from all sides. Water rushes, ocean currents, the flow of the atmosphere.

Then in their shared vision, inharmonious cities spread themselves like rivets over the earth, self-excluded from the flow, they stomp and subdue. Then oceans rise and whales, endless whales.

Mara suddenly feels herself being carried and the depths surge past her as she flies towards the surface. She crests and emerges from the water. Precious air fills her lungs. She gulps it in. The wind whips her hair. She's alive! Alive! More alive than she's ever been before.

And she's riding a whale!

Mara looks down in amazement at the huge whale who's saved her. She lies down on its back and presses her cheek against the gentle beast. And then she cries, letting loose all the emotions that have been building within her.

The beautiful giants carry Tepe and Doctor Zhao too. From wave to wave, the whales shelter the three of them through the storm.

The whales swim so smoothly, and the pod gives a long cascading call, a pure sound that rises in pitch, and then spills down before it lifts again.

"You're an angel!" Mara says, and kisses the whale.

Tepe shouts to Doctor Zhao, "Not even the rain feels cold!".

"The Oracle's potion! I feel the warmth also!" Doctor Zhao shouts back.

As they break out of the clouds, the sun bursts with even more glorious warmth, and for a moment, Mara feels an embrace by something beautiful and vast. *Auntie?* But it's not Auntie, it's something she's never felt before. Mara leans her head against the whale and checks the snap on her front pocket. They were all so close to dying. "It would have been my fault," she whispers.

The storm was fierce, but the waves quickly become calm. And after not too long, Globe Island appears in the distance. Mara can tell it's Globe Island right away because it's a big huge sphere. The huge sphere perches on a foundation of rock like a gigantic grapefruit on a little saucer. The island begins to fill the horizon in front of them.

But as they near, the great whale's voices drop into a mewling melancholy of notes and the humans sink back against their saviors. From the island, the wailing of a thousand voices echoes down the sides and cries into the sea. Doctor Zhao's jaw drops open. Tepe stands, and shields his eyes with his hands. "Oh no," Mara whispers and her body quivers with the overwhelming sorrow she can feel from the island.

The whales swim as close as they can to shore. The three humans take one last moment to hug and rub the backs of the whales. The massive waterborne seem to purr. Then Mara and her friends jump off into the water and swim to a rocky outcropping, where they climb ashore.

The whales whistle goodbye and then they sink back into their ocean home. The humans turn from their saviours and look up towards the island.

Even with the horrible sounds of suffering, it's hard not to notice how beautiful Globe Island is. On the rounded top surface of the island is a thick jungle whose high canopies are pierced by rock formations. As the jungle meets the steeper slopes of the sides of the sphere, the trees begin to stretch horizontally, to reach and grasp at sunlight from beneath their brethren above. Subtle bands of green spread down the sphere as shorter species of trees give way to taller varieties, until the sphere's surface rounds the equator and becomes an under-ceiling, where instead of trees growing up, beardy moss hangs down, down, growing into dense draping swaths of maroon and dark green and drab. The moss weaves through vine formations which hang all the way down to the island's flat foundation below. Mara thinks the island looks like a single scoop ice cream sundae, with dripping sauces and green sprinkles on top, all served on a little flat plate.

But the dripping sauces seem more like tears right now. The screams of anguish from above cause Doctor Zhao's face to twitch and tighten, and Mara's eyes are blurry. Tears flow down her cheeks.

"This is horrible," Doctor Zhao whispers. His thick salt and pepper hair ripples in the breeze. His piercing eyes gaze upwards. "I wonder if the storm blew our two friends with the kites here."

At this Mara shouts, "No!" She rips at her front pocket and tears her sketchbook out and throws it across the rocks. Then she crumples down and grabs her knees and buries her head.

Tepe moves closer and stands next to her. Doctor Zhou walks over and picks up her sketchbook.

He flips through the drawings to her most recent. On the page, the storm that Mara drew is dark and vicious with angry clouds that pelt rain down upon unforgiving waves.

Chapter 9: Consequences

The weeping of Globe Island is the most overwhelming feeling Mara has ever felt in her whole life. It seers through her skin like a thousand needles. It pounds on her heart like a million hammers. And she caused it all, she caused it all!

Doctor Zhao walks over and squats down next to her, holding her sketchbook open to her drawing of the storm. "Mara, you drew this on the boat?"

She grinds her head into her knees, "It's all my fault!"

He pats her on the shoulder. "No wonder you're here," he says. "Mara, you have a great talent. Just like Auntie."

Somehow, her sadness recedes enough for her to turn her head a little and look at him with one teary eye. *What is he talking about?* she thinks to herself.

Doctor Zhao asks her, "How do you think your aunt was able to create this house?"

She shrugs, and wipes at her eyes.

Doctor Zhao sits down next to her. "I was going to let Auntie explain all this, but… Well, you see, there are rare people in this world who can do extraordinary things. Like you and your Aunt."

"I thought Auntie just designed the house and people came and built it. But maybe... Didn't people build it?"

Doctor Zhao shakes his head. "Many people are helping to fix what your Aunt created because things didn't quite happen like she planned. Let's just say she overextended herself. A lot. So she's brought in some very talented artists and engineers and scientists to help make everything better, but it's an absolutely enormous task we have."

"How did she create it though?"

"Magic. Like yours."

Mara's eyes widen, but she knows it to be true. She knows that the weird thing that's happened with her drawings—the river, the storm—magic! She nods for Doctor Zhao to continue.

"The Designer has the magical talent called 'Creation.' She can actually create real things. And I believe you have this talent also, because it seems you created that storm with your drawing."

Mara frowns and looks up towards the top of the island. The wailing has grown louder. She shudders.

Doctor Zhao continues, "Mara, I saw the purple sparks, the sparks are one of the signs of a talent being used."

"I could feel it."

"I'm sure you could. What's most interesting to me is that you're using the same technique as your aunt—you draw."

"How does it work?" Mara asks.

Doctor Zhao shifts a bit to face her. "Auntie will be able to explain to you better than me, but she says doing magic is like feeling a deep emotion."

"Do you have magic too?"

Doctor Zhao shakes his head. "No, I'm just a normal guy who's pretty good at making models."

"I like your models. Um… You called it creation, a talent… But Doctor Zhao, I don't know how to use the magic. I'm hurting people. I almost killed us in the ocean, and now this island is weeping and I just know it's my fault."

"Mara, don't blame yourself, you were trying to help us."

She wipes her eyes dry. "Will everything I draw become real?"

He shakes his head no. "Only the drawings you want to become real will. Auntie says there's a difference between creativity and creation." He sets her sketchbook down on the stone next to her. "Are you ready to find out what's going up there? Whatever's happening, we need to try and help."

"Yes. Let's help." She glances at her sketchbook. "But I'm not gonna draw in it."

"You don't have to."

She pushes herself up with her hands. Then, standing over her book, she looks up at the top of the island again. The weeping is like huge melting snowflakes.

Mara reaches down and grabs her sketchbook, then she stuffs it away and snaps her front pocket shut.

"Okay good," Doctor Zhao says. "You ready now?"

"Ya," she nods. Except her sketchbook feels a lot heavier.

Tepe leads the way across the stone plates of the saucer-like base of the island until they reach the patchwork curtain of vines which mark the outer edge of the mossy subterior of the globe. The hanging vines have grown as thick and strong as millennial sequoia. Groupings of these vines create upside-down skyscrapers. Tendrils creep down from on high, but broad leaves mask the view above.

Doctor Zhao's face is drawn as he searches above. "It sounds truly terrible. Tepe, can you find us a way up?"

"Already looking," Tepe says.

Tepe leads them around the base, running his hands over the gatherings of vines. Several times, he climbs up into the tumbling cascades, but on these first occasions, he quickly drops back down and describes a tangle, or an overhang.

Finally, they find the scuffs and smoothings of human passage on a group of vines that's thick and dense as far up as they can see.

Tepe scrabbles up to scout.

Mara and Doctor Zhao wait for him. But suddenly, after a minute or two, a violent cough erupts from the undergrowth next them.

Doctor Zhao and Mara both stumble back a few steps. "Was that a person?" Mara whispers.

"Ya, it sounded that way," Doctor Zhao whispers back. Then he says to the undergrowth, "H..hello?"

The breeze scrapes across the rocks and hisses underneath

the shifting vegetation.

He asks again, "Hello? Is someone there?"

The undergrowth is dead quiet, and nothing moves for a moment.

But then again, with sudden ferocity, ragged coughing quakes the moss.

"Oh my," Doctor Zhao says.

He and Mara take a few more steps back.

"Ah... Are you okay?" Mara asks. "Please come out."

A boy's voice, all contorted, yells out, "You go!" But the boy can't hold back his coughing anymore. He explodes into a choking fit and stumbles out of the moss. Coughing and staggering, he crumbles to the ground in front of them.

Mara starts to rush right towards him, but Doctor Zhao grabs her arm.

"What?" Mara asks, pulling to get free.

"Wait Mara. He's sick. Look at his skin, we need to keep our distance," Doctor Zhao says.

The boy's wearing a suit of sores. He's coiled up around his hands, jolting with the explosions in his lungs.

"Oh no..." Mara whispers. "No, no, no." She balls her fists. Shudders run through her. "This can't be, this can't be."

"Hold it together Mara." Doctor Zhao pats his coat pockets. "Okay, okay, um... We need to somehow get in touch with the infirmary. We need to..."

But then Mara remembers the words of the Oracle. She

hears the words singing in her mind, *Health embraces disease.* She knows she should keep her distance from sick people, but this time something is different. The Oracle's words echo louder and louder in her thoughts. This time she somehow knows that she needs to embrace this boy. She dashes towards him.

"No! Mara!" Doctor Zhao leaps, but he can't catch her. Mara spills to the ground and grabs the boy into a big hug.

"I'm so sorry," she says. "I'm so sorry."

The boy groans in her arms.

Just then, Tepe hops down. "What's going... Oh whoa, Doctor Zhao?"

Doctor Zhao has horror and revulsion and concern all mixed together on his face as he watches Mara cradle the sick boy. He doesn't even know how to respond to Tepe.

But then Doctor Zhao's eyes suddenly get really wide and he gasps, "What's that now?"

A faint green burbling glow has appeared where Mara's hands are holding the boy's arms, and the boy seems to be easing a bit. The glow is like a simmering iridescent algae.

Mara feels a strong tingling in her hands and she gasps and opens her eyes. "What's that? Oh wow!"

"It's the same color as the gas in the Oracle's vials," Tepe points out.

"It feels tingly and warm," Mara says.

Doctor Zhao nods. "It is the same green." He pulls out a magnifying glass and moves closer.

The boy's shivering subsides. He quiets and begins to breathe more smoothly.

Doctor Zhao exclaims, "What?... Oh my...Oh...I...Oh my..."

Tepe looks over Doctor Zhao's shoulder through the glass. "What are those?"

"What is it?" Mara asks

"There's... There appears to be lots of... I can barely see them with this glass—lots of tiny little creatures hopping from you to him. They're just scrambling out of your skin they're so tiny. They've got four unusually jointed limbs, and they're sort of tumbling. And they dive right into this poor boy's skin. Oh, and yes, they're glowing green."

"I think it's making him better," Mara says. "Please get better."

The boy is getting better. His breathing grows deeper and steadier. They can see that the green creatures have spread throughout his body because all over him, even on his feet, his sores shine green as they heal and dry and close as they watch. The fiery lines on his skin fade into the green glow.

"Put your hands on him Doctor Zhao," Mara whispers.

"Uh… Oh.... I guess I did drink the Oracle's potion also. Hmm. Okay, well..." He closes his eyes, turns his head away, and then places his hand on the boy's arm.

"Am I ok? Am I ok?"

"Look Doctor Zhao." Mara can't help but giggle at him. "Health embraces disease."

Doctor Zhao peeks one eye open. The green glow has appeared where he's making contact. After a moment, he whispers, "Health embraces disease. The Oracle gave us the cure. This is a miracle!"

Tepe turns his hand back and forth several times, then he reaches it out and places it on the boy's forehead. At his touch too, the green glow shines.

The boy's eyelids flutter open.

Mara pats him. "It's okay, you're okay."

His eyes grow large and he gapes up at Mara. "I'm okay! I feel better!" Then he asks her, "Are you a goddess?"

She giggles, pushes him out of her arms and hops to her feet. "Get up silly." Then, "Hey, can you show us the way up? We want to help everyone."

The boy jumps to his feet. "Yes! Thank you! It's right here." He runs to the grouping of vines that Tepe was scouting. "Up this way!"

Then they climb after the boy. And they climb, and climb. Straight up sturdy ladders woven from the living vines, the group is muted by the effort of the ascent. They traverse ramps and wind up spirals, and when the vines grow sparse again, they're back to scaling ladder-like weavings. Strong winds blend the salt of the ocean and the musk of the moss, but the ladders barely sway.

Up and up, Tepe and the young islander sometimes get far ahead and have to check back on Doctor Zhao and Mara.

"I'm fine, keep going," Mara says. She trudges upwards,

numb from the effort, and also numbing herself to the song of sadness from on high. It's too much to feel. But they're bringing the cure she hopes. One foot, then the next. Hand over hand. Step by step.

Finally they near the equator of the globe and they start to climb through the sideways canopies of wild fig trees, whose deep roots allow them to grow straight out from the waist of the island.

The weeping grows louder as they round the equator.

"My goodness," Doctor Zhao says.

"We're almost there," Mara whispers under her breath.

The climbing evolves into steep crawling, then they're actually walking up a steep path. And soon enough the trees are growing straight up out of the ground. The boy leads them through majestic kapoks which soar high over the paperbarks and strangler figs. The moths don't seem to notice the sounds of the weeping island, but the birds are quiet. They quickly flit from branch to branch when they need to move. Mara can feel thick layers of leaves under her shoes, and even the air is earthy.

After a little ways they come across a sick and unconscious woman lying in the path. Mara pushes past the others, kneels down and holds the woman's hands in hers.

"It's working again!" she says as the green glow appears. "This is good, this is good."

Tepe and Doctor Zhao place their hands on the woman's shoulders and from them too, the tiny green creatures migrate and dance. The woman's breathing quickly calms.

Tepe looks up at the young islander who's staring at them with his jaw dropped open. "Come on!" Tepe says to him.

The boy kneels, then touches the woman's arm.

"Ayy!" he exclaims as the glow appears. "It tickles!"

"The healing creatures are in him too. He can cure people too now. This is very good," Doctor nods at Mara.

The woman's sores heal and her shivering subsides. She sits up with a start and scrambles backwards at first, but then she sees the boy. "Gari...how did...we're better?"

"Yes, we're better." He pulls her to her feet.

Mara hops up also. Her face is bright. "Come on. We have to heal everyone."

"Yes!" Tepe says.

"Excellent!" Doctor Zhou claps. "We must spread the cure as fast as we can!"

Mara says, "Imagine it's a huge game of healing tag and we're it, okay?" Then she turns and sprints off.

The group rushes along on the path after her, and at the first village they fan out and heal the groaning sick as they come upon them.

"I love the green things!" Mara yells over to Doctor Zhao. The man she's healing stirs and jumps up. "Tag! Your it!" Mara says. "Now go heal someone!" And she runs to the next person she can find.

The glowing of the tumbly creatures, like a wave, flows through the village as the healing spreads exponentially. Each sick person that's cured joins the ranks of healers, and soon, all of the villages on Globe Island are healthy and whole again.

In joy, voices rise and bodies dance. Globe Island no longer weeps, now it sings!

Feet hop, hands clap! Drums pound, chants sound!

Hug ground! Hug trees!

Tumble, rumble, bob, bowl!

Green glow, heal me whole!

Green glow! Heal me whole!

"They tumble like this!" the boy Gari shouts and then he cartwheels through the dance. A stream of screaming kids flip heads over heels after him.

The people of the island, with Mara and her friends, celebrate in the central village at the very top of Globe Island. Cavern homes echo song, and treetop houses boom with drums. Elders wave down from walkways in the trees.

Mara hops and stomps and laughs and shouts. Doctor Zhou claps and smiles.

Tepe suddenly tumbles up a tree and all the kids scream with delight. He pops from branch to branch, to vine and then swings around. Hop, hop, hop, swing! Villagers join him and soon the canopy soars and swoops and sings.

But then, in the midst of the celebration, a few young men and women with spears run up to Mara.

"We found the bad people in the woods. They're really sick."

"Oh no!" Mara says. She rushes the group over to Doctor Zhao.

"Where are they?" Doctor Zhao asks.

A woman answers, "Into the jungle a little ways. The two of them look like each other." The woman leads them away from the dance and back into the woods. They follow a path until the woman breaks off and pushes through the rough. Mara can see ripped fragments of kite fluttering in the trees overhead.

The woman stops them. Then they peek through the bushes.

The two soldiers lay tangled and motionless where they crash landed. They lay in a disorderly nest of broken branches, ferns and twisted rope.

"They're twins," Doctor Zhou says.

"Are they dead?" Mara asks.

"Let's go check." Doctor Zhao climbs over the tangle, kneels down and checks the pulse of one of the soldiers. "Oh! Not necessary I guess." He says as the green glow appears at his touch.

Mara and the woman kneel next to the other man and grab his hands. "The green creatures are tumbling here too," Mara says.

"Okay you two," Doctor Zhao says, "when they wake up, we're going to jump away."

They both nod. "Okay," Mara says.

The four other villagers move closer, spears ready.

"The Oracle knew," Doctor Zhao says. "And Mara, you were brave enough to embrace Gari. You made it happen! Oh wait, what's this?" He pulls a knife from the soldier's ankle holster and tosses it into the woods. The woman kneeling with Mara does the same for the other soldier.

Doctor Zhao says, "I don't see any more weapons, but what's in this greasy shoulder pocket here?" He goes to unzip the pocket, and as his hand nears, a brilliant beam of the tiny green creatures flashes from his hand and charges at the pocket. "Whoa!" Doctor Zhao says.

"Wow," Mara echoes. The pocket boils bright green.

"Perhaps the source of the disease?" Doctor Zhao says. After the boil settles to a simmer, he unzips the pocket and pulls out a dented steel case. Inside are five crushed glass tubes, each holding a small piece of fabric. The creatures swarm over the broken glass and the scraps of fabric. Doctor Zhao clicks his tongue. "This is quite bad. They brought disease with them. I didn't think the invaders could be capable of such an atrocity."

The twins stir at almost the same time. Their eyelids flutter, and they groan.

"Come on,' Doctor Zhou warns. He and Mara and the woman jump back behind the other four villagers who point their spears at the two invaders.

The twins open their eyes, and like one, they gasp, assess each other, glance around, and then they leap up into snarling crouches.

"Easy, easy," Doctor Zhou says.

The one twin slaps his shoulder pocket. Then he screams,

"Oh my god, we're all gonna die!"

"Hold on! Hold on!" Doctor Zhao says. "Your diseases have been cured." He holds up the steel case.

"What? What?" The soldier scans everyone, and then feels his face. "How did… This was an accident!" He raises his hands. "Accident! We don't use this kind of thing against innocents. You gotta believe me! At least me and my brother don't." His brother nods.

"We surrender," the first twin says, and holds up his hands. "We're done with this contract. Ain't seen nothing but nice people here. You gotta understand, I'm Craig and this is my brother, Greg, and we work for thieves, but we only steal from thieves. It's our code! And you all are not corporate pirates, at all. You're all like a fantasy land or something. So we surrender!"

"Yup," his brother Greg says. "Just like a fantasy. We definitely surrender!"

"Okay," Doctor Zhao says. "Well, if you could just stay inside the ring of spears while we head back to the village, that would be great."

"No problem, understood." The two hold up their hands.

The group makes their way back, and when they arrive, the dancers part for them. The villagers pause their celebration to point and whisper at the twins.

"Gosh, the twins actually seem to feel bad," Mara says to Doctor Zhao.

"Yes, I'm a bit surprised really. An interesting response to the house."

"It is like a fantasy land."

"I suppose so." Doctor Zhou nods.

Tepe and Gari run over, and looking at the twins, Gari says, "I'm glad everyone's all right. Doctor Zhou, Mara, would you follow Tepe and I up to meet with our elders?"

"Lead the way," Doctor Zhao says.

They leave the twins to wait on the ground. Gari guides Mara, Doctor Zhao and Tepe up ramps and across walkways through the trees. They go higher and higher into the canopy. The walkways sway and Mara giggles. "This is really high."

Doctor Zhao keeps his chin up. "I'm not looking down, thank you."

They pass people's homes. They cross over cooking platforms. The villagers make way for them and smile and wave.. A little monkey hops up to Mara's shoulder. "Hi there!" she says and puts her finger up. The little monkey grabs it with its hand and shakes it.

A young girl runs out of a nearby treehouse. "Oh he likes you!" She holds her arms up and the little monkey hops over to her and sits on the little girl's shoulder.

"He's so cute," Mara says. "I love him."

"Maybe come back and play?" the girl asks.

"I will," Mara says. "As soon as I can."

The girl nods and joins her older brother who waves at them from his perch on a railing.

Finally, Gari leads them up a set of stairs which spirals around the huge trunk of one of the tallest kapoks, and they ascend through the jungle canopy into the sunlight and it seems like they are standing on top of the world. Their eyes adjust to the brightness as they step up onto a large round platform.

Three elders sit on pillows. They look as old as the moon, a woman in the center, and a man and another woman at her sides.

The platform they inhabit is shaped from the uppermost branches of the majestic tree, Doctor Zhou bends down to one knee and feels the living floor. The branches have been grown into an expanding sunwise spiral, close and layered, not a gap or crack to be found. Mara holds her hand over her brow and steps onto one of the soft grass sitting mats that are scattered across the surface.

Low tables are spaced around the edge of the platform and they're filled with statues and stones, crystals, little plants flourishing in shells and husks, dried plants, mushrooms, fragments of wood. The statues are formed from all different materials, and are all different shapes. There are statues of little flora and fauna, or simple triangles, circles, there's even little scenes with tiny people casting nets from canoes or crouching with spears by a young deer that was born with a weak leg.

Below the edges of the platform, the canopy spreads out and falls away with the curve of Globe Island, and in all directions, the ocean reaches into the horizon.

The sun cries it's rays over them with a gentle late morning gold, but it keeps glinting sharply off of an object directly into

Mara's eyes. She puts her other hand over her brow also and squints.

She takes a few steps towards the bright object, it's like a star, a mini sun sitting on the table. She squints until she can barely see at all, and takes two more stuttering steps forward.

"Gari, help her," says the very old woman who sits in the center of the three elders.

Gari crosses to Mara, and holds her elbow to steady her. "Mara, what are you doing? You're stumbling towards the edge."

"There's something on the table there," Mara says. "Isn't it sparkling at you?"

"Take her over there," the old woman says.

"Okay, yes Maman," Gari says. "Point again?"

Mara does and he helps her cross to the table. "Ya," she says.

At the table, Mara puts her hands in front of her eyes and tries to peek through her fingers. "It's as bright as the sun. I can't look at it."

"Take it," the old woman says in her gruff, creaking voice. The three elders fix their wrinkled gazes upon Mara.

Mara bends her knees a bit and feels her hand through the air until her fingers run into the object. She yanks back at first, but then feels forward again and takes a hold of it.

She cups it in front of her and cracks her left eye. "It's not sparkly anymore."

She pushes the grape-sized stone around in her palm with a

98

finger. "It looks like a heart, it's so detailed, it looks real."

"Bring it here," the woman says.

Mara crosses over and hands it to her. The woman bounces it around in her crinkled palm, then smells it, holds it against her cheek. "I shall miss this," she whispers. "I've held it often since it was brought here."

Then she presses the heart back into Mara's hand. "What's your name?"

"I'm Mara."

"Well you must be someone very special Mara."

Mara blushes, and frowns just a little.

The woman's eyes twinkle and she smiles. "Not so sure about yourself yet?" She pats Mara's hands. "All things with time. Safeguard this heart. It is very important to the woman who brought it here. She called the heart 'The first part of the key.'"

"Really?" Mara's eyes get really big.

"I'm approaching please." Doctor Zhao bobs with his hands out and then rushes over.

"The woman?" Mara asks.

"The woman that saved us from the loud birds that shook the sky. The birds were bothering us, but then the sky blurred and the stars changed, and then the birds were gone and she appeared. She wore a dress covered in flowers, and with open arms, she seemed to embrace the whole world."

"That's my aunt!" Mara says. "What else did she say?"

"Many things." The old woman pushes up to her feet and

the two other elders stand also. "Come though, we need to go down." The woman takes Mara's hand and they make their way to the stairs.

The whole group spirals back down, sways along walkways, descends ramps and ladders till they get to the forest floor. The spearmen still wait with the twin kite-surfers, Craig and Greg.

"These are the mirrors you saved us from?" the old woman asks Mara.

Mara nods.

Craig drops to his knees and puts his hands together. "Grandmother, can you forgive us?"

He pulls his brother Greg down next to him. "We meant no harm,"

Greg nods, "We only steal from thieves like ourselves."

"No innocents! That's our motto," Craig says.

"That's our motto," his brother repeats.

"We wouldn't have signed up for this if we'd known."

"No way."

Doctor Zhou interrupts them, "Who do you work for?"

The twins shrink a bit.Greg glances into the woods. "You don't want to know," he says.

Craig slaps a fly off his forehead. "I got no clue what you got here, but when they called for the job... whew! The hairs on my arms stood straight up. Bottom line—rich."

Greg nods fiercely. "The crew—pro."

"So we were in for sure. But you've got The Lady Banks up in here. It's not just her though, a whole grip of bosses. Grove, The Brothers K, Ms. Pfiz, L. Martin, all here."

"Oh my!" Doctor Zhao says.

"You know who we're talking about?" Greg asks.

"No, not really. Well, yes, perhaps I've heard the names before." Doctor Zhao touches his nose.

"Then you know," Craig says. "We've worked for them all, over the years. One against the other even, but I've never seen them team up like this. What're you hiding here?"

"I honestly don't know," Doctor Zhao says.

"Well they're going to get it, whatever it is. I guarantee that," Craig says.

"No they won't!" Mara yells.

Greg shakes his head. "I'm sorry little girl, but they will. My best advice—run."

Mara tries to storm off, but the old woman holds her hand tight. "Oops," Mara says as she catches her feet and stumbles back against the old woman. "Sorry."

"We have somewhere to be," the old woman says. And turning from the twins, she pulls Mara along.

Doctor Zhao throws up his hands. "Can't we ask them a few more questions?"

But the old man grabs his arm and says, "No more answers here."

Craig speaks up, "Wait, can we stay here?"

The elders lead Mara and her friends away, out of the village.

Greg calls after, "We can't go back, we can help!"

The elders ignore them. The guards ignore them. Mara looks back at the twins, who have dropped to their knees, imploring. Then the path turns and the leaves of the jungle swallow her view.

"What will happen to them?" Mara asks.

The old woman trudges forward. "They'll learn to live here, or they'll leave on a boat," she says.

"Oh. That's not so bad."

"Perhaps they're refugees now from their former life," Maman says and gives Mara's hand a squeeze.

The group walks along the sloping path. Birds whistle and sing again, and a nice wind urges the trees to caress each other, so they rub and whisper.

A ways down, the old woman finally stops and gestures at an overgrown scrap of trail that's been blocked with wild logs. "Down there, your aunt showed us a cavern. It was not there before she arrived. 'The cavern is only for those who come from across the waters,' your aunt said. We don't enter."

"Why not?" Doctor Zhao asks.

"Uncomfortable."

Maman turns to Mara and takes her other hand. "Mara dear, will you ask your aunt to visit us?"

Mara nods. "I will. Um, thank you for your help."

"Gari told us how you had the courage to hold him, to discover that you could heal us. It's we who must thank you."

Mara blushes. "No, I…"

But Gari steps forward and gives her a quick hug. "I hope you come back to visit." He brushes the hair out of his face. "Cause I'm gonna miss you." He turns away quickly.

"Wait!" Mara says.

She reaches for the snap on her pocket, but then freezes and looks down. "Oh ya..." she mutters.

"It's okay Mara," Doctor says.

"Mmmm, okay," she says. Mara wrinkles her face around and unsnaps her pocket. Then she shakes her hair. "Okay," she says again and pulls out her sketchbook.

"I just..." She flips through the first thirty drawings or so, and then backs up a couple pages. She pulls her purple pencil out, stares at it for a moment, then she goes ahead and puts it to the page. She writes in the corner, then stuffs her pencil back into her pocket.

"Um, I wanted to give you this." She folds the inner edge of the page back and forth several times and then licks along the fold. She carefully tears the page out of her sketchbook.

"Here." She hands it to him.

Gari looks at her drawing, then says, "Wow!" The elders lean over to see.

"It's a planet I made up called Fuguu where turtle people live," Mara says.

Gari reads the corner, "Till we meet again Gari, my best wishes, Mara." He smiles at her. "I can't wait. And Mara, this drawing is amazing! These islands...with all the different plants and animals, and look at the turtle people, they're so cool. Their little shell shaped villages. This close up of the inside of one of their homes is really neat."

The old man points over Gari's shoulder, "Look, they collect water with those large leaves."

"And here are kelp cities off the coast," Gari says.

"They have a box that lifts them up the cliff?" the old man asks.

Mara nods, "That's an elevator. Here's a closeup of the pulley mechanism."

"A pulley," the old man mutters.

"I really like it Mara," Gari says. "I really like it."

"It's all right." Mara shrugs.

The old woman pats Gari's shoulder. "We were asked not to delay the heart."

"Oh, okay." Gari turns to Mara. "Bye Mara."

"Bye Gari."

There are more goodbyes, until the old woman claps her hands. "Down the path now, the cavern's not far."

Mara scrabbles over the logs blocking the unused path and pushes the leaves out of the way. Doctor Zhou follows her over, but Tepe doesn't.

"Tepe?" Mara says.

Tepe stands next to the second old woman, who has her hand on his shoulder.

"You're going to stay?" Doctor Zhao asks.

Tepe nods.

He springs over and hugs Mara and Doctor Zhao, then he bounces back to Gari and the elders of Globe Island.

Tepe has found his home.

Chapter 10: Descent

"The cavern's over here," Mara says.

"That wasn't far." Doctor Zhao rounds the trunk of the huge kapok tree. "Oh my, how beautiful."

"Auntie designed this, I can tell," Mara says. She hops up on a rock. Across from her is the cavern entrance tucked into the hollow of a giant tree. Dew, still glistening around the shaded hollow, sends light sparkling across her face. Little drips of the gentle water slide slowly down the vines which embrace the kapok. They reach the fringe topping the opening of the cavern, and then lazily fall from the fine tendrils, forming a curtain of drops that flows into the mossy rocks below.

"It reminds me of Seergart's grotto," Mara says.

"Oh yes." Doctor Zhao nods. He steps down to the entrance and peers inside. "The tunnel looks pretty straight."

"Is it dark?" Mara asks.

"Not near the entrance. But further in it is."

"Hmmm." Mara frowns.

"I'm sure it'll be okay." He steps through the fine veil of water, then wipes his face dry. "Come on."

"Will you hold my hand if it gets really dark?" Mara asks.

"Of course I will Mara."

"Okay." She brushes her fingers against the smooth edges of the tree's hollow as she passes through the curtain of dew and into the cavern.

Doctor Zhao leads the way. "It's quite a nice sized tunnel."

Their shadows run far ahead as the daylight spills past them.

Mara's never walked through a tunnel before. And this one goes under an ocean, so it must be very long. It might get small, and there doesn't seem to be any light ahead of them. They might have to walk through the darkness. Mara reaches out and grabs Doctor Zhao's hand in her own.

"You're a very brave person." Doctor Zhao says to her. "This is quite the adventure we're on."

Mara giggles, "I don't think I'm very brave." But just then, she notices something on the left wall of the cavern ahead of them. "What's that?" Mara points with her free hand.

"I'm not sure, it looks like a big carving of some sort," Doctor Zhao says.

As they approach, they see that the jumble of shaped rocks on the side of the wall creates a rugged face. The individual stones that make up it's eyes and nose and mouth seem to be well embedded into the cavern wall. It's got stern eyebrows and plump cheeks. While they're examining it's features, the craggy face suddenly comes alive and yells at them, "THE KEY!"

Mara and Doctor Zhao stumble back. "Oh my goodness!"

Doctor Zhao yells. "Ahh!" Mara screams and latches onto his forearm.

The Lady Banks' mean voice laughs at them. "Come here you twits."

As they regain their footing, Doctor Zhao whispers to Mara, "This face must be one of our intercoms."

Mara shakes her finger at the face, "Stop yelling so much!"

The face glares and them. Then it sneers, "The key…" The Lady Banks hisses. "Bring me the key…. Doctor Zhao, who is your silly friend? Do you know what we'll do if you don't find the key? We're going to tie The Designer to the vault door and then we're going to blow it all to smithereens."

"NO!!" Mara cries out. "Don't hurt Auntie!! Please! We're gonna find it! We already found part of it!"

"Part of the key?" The Lady Banks asks eagerly.

"Yes!" Mara says.

"Mara wait," Doctor Zhao says, but Mara already holds the little heart up high.

The beady stone eyes examine it intensely. "This is just part of it?!"

"Yes." Mara nods. The heart catches traces of daylight and shines in her hand. "Is Auntie okay? Where are you? Why are you doing…"

But The Lady Banks cuts her off, "Where is the rest of the key?"

"Why are you so mean?" Mara cries out. "Why don't you

just go home! Just leave us…"

"The keeeyyy," The Lady Banks hisses again.

Mara frowns. She clamps the heart to her chest and growls. Doctor Zhao puts his hand on her shoulder. "We're looking for the rest right now. But we need you to call off your goons."

"THE KEY DOCTOR ZHAO!"

"Ahh!" Doctor Zhao stumbles back again, but Mara catches his hand and manages to help him stay upright.

"Stop that!" she scolds the stone face. "I want to talk to Auntie!"

"Oh my." Doctor Zhao smoothes his lapels. "That's just horrible."

"Where's Auntie?" Mara yells.

The stone face, unmoving now, glares and stares.

"Now Lady Banks," Doctor Zhao says, "I'll ask again if you could please call off your soldiers?" He waves his hand at Mara, who holds back her next outburst.

After a moment, Doctor Zhao says, "Are you still there?"

The bulbous eyes of the face on the wall are cracked a bit and the protruding mouth is still slightly open.

"Lady Banks?" Doctor Zhao asks again.

Mara steps towards the face. "Did you leave?" Then to Doctor Zhao, "Did she leave? That's not fair." She stomps her foot. "That's not fair Doctor Zhao!"

"Come on Mara." He holds his hand out. With a harrumph, she grabs it and the two of them head further into the tunnel.

Mara fumes as the hard earth descends steeply into the darkness.

Eventually though, the last creeping particles of light from the entrance lose their will, and as the darkness deepens, Mara slows down.

"Are you okay?" Doctor Zhao asks.

She stops, she can barely see her hand when she holds it all the way out. "I don't think so," she says. In the dark, there might be a cliff, or monsters, or bats, or anything really. There could be alien mole people down here with no eyes at all and their big noses can smell everything. There could be...

"Do you want me to search ahead quickly?" Doctor Zhao asks.

"No!" She grabs his sleeve. "I want to stay with you."

"Of course, of course." He takes one step forward. But then he stops and says, "Mara, you could make us some light if you want."

"What do you...Oh!" She reaches up and touches her sketchbook with her free hand. She moves her lips back and forth. "I don't know if that's a good idea, let's just go ahead."

"Okay," he says. "I'll touch the wall here and we'll head forward."

"I'm gonna hold your hand and I'm not gonna let go."

"Deal."

They walk forward until it's so perfectly dark that their eyes serve no purpose at all. Mara can't tell if having her eyes open is scarier than closing her eyes. She tries both. She tries one eye closed and one eye open. Her heart keeps beating faster and faster though.

The shuffle of their feet, their breathing, the quiet little sounds that they can't hide echo off the walls of the tunnel. Mara shivers. Doctor Zhao squeezes her hand.

"We're doing fine," he says, right as he and Mara step onto something slick. Mara's foot slips back, and she flops forward, pulling Doctor Zhao down with her. His feet fly out in front of him and he lands on his butt. "Oof!"

Then they both start sliding down the slippery surface.

"Whoaaaaaa!" Doctor Zhao struggles to stop them. "It's algae or something! I can't get a grip. Mara, spin around, get your head up here, we might run into something."

As they slide faster, she unwraps from his leg, flips around and clings onto his arm instead.

"Doctor Zhao…" Mara whispers with fear.

"I hope we're gonna be okay Mara, just hold on."

They slide and slide, very straight. The ground is smooth and they're barely descending, but the sheen of wet algae is as slick as glazed porcelain. So they begin to go faster and faster.

This slide is almost as terrible as the one with Chawz, but at least Mara's with Doctor Zhao this time. Seergart saved her then.

She begins to hum. She tries to find that tone that Seergart taught her about. And after a few stutters, she finds it! She finds that tone which resonates through her whole body. She knows it's her sacred tone because she becomes much calmer when she finds it.

Doctor Zhao begins to hum also. It's obvious that he already knows his tone, because he finds it right away. It's lower. Humming together, their chord fills the tunnel and for a moment, the slide feels peaceful.

But only moments later, Doctor Zhao stops and says, "Mara, open your eyes."

"A tiny light is coming at us!" she says. She readjusts so she can see better. It's like a star getting bigger and bigger, coming right at them.

"Actually, I think we're approaching it," Doctor Zhao says.

The light grows, and grows, until it brightens the ceiling.

"Actually I think it's a hole in the floor." Doctor Zhao scrabbles fruitlessly to slow them down. Mara tries to dig in her heels, but that doesn't help.

"Hold on Mara! We're gonna fall through!"

Chapter 11: Representation

Mara and Doctor Zhao slide towards the growing light at the end of the tunnel. The hole waiting to swallow them.

"Aaahh!" Mara screams.

But they can't stop themselves. With slipping feet and flailing arms, they drop right through the hole and into the daytime.

"Whooooaaaaa!" Doctor Zhao yells.

Blinded by daylight, they fall through the air. Then they splash into a well of water.

Mara can't believe this is happening again. She kicks to the surface and grabs onto the rocky edge nearby. Gasping, the light is so bright still, she blurts out, "Another well!?"

Doctor Zhao clings to the edge next to her. He rubs the water from his eyes and looks up. "Oh my! What's this?"

A whole bunch of medieval guards in plate mail armor are gaping at them with dropped jaws and wide eyes.

Mara and Doctor Zhao stare back from the well, equally shocked. They're in some sort of courtyard, with some sort of King. Mara rubs her eyes and takes a second look. Ya, that's definitely a King on a throne.

"SEIZE THEM!" the King shouts, his face twists furiously. He leaps onto his throne and whips his scepter around and points it at the interlopers. "SEIZE THEM!" he roars again, with a booming voice.

"Oh no..." Doctor Zhao groans. The guards jump at the king's order. They leap forward and drag Doctor Zhao and Mara out of the pool and flop them onto the floor.

"Hey!" Mara yells.

The King jumps on his throne. "APPOINT THEM THE ROLE OF... PRISONER! PRISONER!" He slashes his scepter at them, and kicks the air. "DUNGEONS! TO THE DUNGEONS! CORRUPTORS OF OUR UPSIDE DOWN WELL! DEEPEST DARKEST DUNGEONS!"

The guards holler and tussle. "Over here!" "Up there!" "Get them!" "Grab them!"

"Noo!" Mara cries. "What are you..Hey!"

Doctor Zhao crabs backwards. "Wait! Listen to us. Please!"

The King roars, "GET THEM OUT! OUT! NOW I SAY! GET THEM TO THE LOWEST MOST DISGUSTING DUNGEON IN THE KINGDOM WHERE THEY'LL BE FORGOTTEN ABOUT!"

The guards jolt, they jostle, then all at once, they grab Doctor Zhao and Mara. They lift them into the air and hold them tight above their heads, and the smooshed pack careens away.

"Let go of my ear!" Doctor Zhao shouts.

Mara squirms and squiggles, but the platform of hands has

her locked. "Shoot," she says and stops struggling. She catches her breath, stares up at the sky, and tries to hum her sacred tone. It's too shaky though!

The guards clatter across a large grassy area that faces the throne, then they crash through the gates of a small stone wall that encloses the grass and the court.

Doctor Zhao gets his head free enough to be able to look around a bit. "Some sort of kingdom, in a valley," he mutters. Surrounding the valley on all sides are massive white shouldered mountain peaks that soar upwards to meet the sky. Behind them, the throne room shelters under a jutting overhang at the foot of the mountains.

The guards clang through a marketplace now. They stomp past covered stands where peasants stop their work and gawk.

"Peasants?" Doctor Zhao says.

Mara doesn't want to think about disgusting dungeons, so she watches a swarm of blackbirds bubble and turn in the sky and she tries not to freak out. Her sketchbook is snapped tight. *Dungeons?!*

The cluster of armored soldiers holding their prisoners above their heads clammers out of the market and passes through groups of scattered huts which huddle under the ash trees. Grubby people inside the huts peer out of their windows and doorways at the jumbling commotion.

But then, suddenly, a really loud bell starts ringing: "Bn-Bong, BONG, Bong, bn-BONG…"

And in a crashing halt, the guards just drop Doctor Zhao and Mara right on top of themselves. The whole jumble tumbles into a heap. "Oof!" "Ow!"

After a moment of untangling, everyone crabbles up to their feet

The bell keeps ringing, "BONG-bn, BONGG!..."

The guards casually wipe themselves down and stroll off, back in the direction of the king's court.

"What's this?" Doctor Zhao says.

Out of the houses too, people wrap scarves around their heads, throw capes over their shoulders, and head towards the throne.

Doctor Zhao and Mara stand there as the guards walk away.

"Doctor Zhao, what's happening?" Mara asks.

He purses his eyes a little. After a moment's consideration, he says, "Now that's pretty weird. Maybe we should follow them and find out what's going on."

"I don't want to be in a disgusting dungeon..."

"No, no, neither do I," Doctor Zhao says. "We'll stay hidden, come on." He crouches down and creeps after the crowd.

"All right," Mara whispers. She copies Doctor Zhao and drops into a creeping stance, looks left and right, then follows.

They make their way back through the huts and then the market stands. It's totally deserted, they could have stormed through on rhinos. Nonetheless, they creep. They creep all the way back to the chest-high stone wall surrounding the field in front of the king's court. Then they peek over the top of the wall, just as the bell stops its bonging.

The whole town stands gathered on the grass in front of the court. The king is gone, the dais is empty, the throne stands lonely. The only movement up there is the drip, drip, drip of water into the well from the overhang above, the upside down well as the king called it.

As the bell stops, the crowd settles. "Looks like about a hundred peasants," Doctor Zhao says quietly.

"Ya, but where's the king?" Mara whispers. "Look, something's happening."

A woman walks out of the crowd and steps up onto the dais. "That's not the king," Mara says. "Why is everyone here so dirty? Why are you calling them peasants?"

"Oh I guess I shouldn't call them that, but don't they look like they're from a few hundred years ago?"

"They're all dressed alike," Mara says.

"Not a lot of variety for poor people back then. Okay, she's gonna sit on the throne."

The woman does sit on the throne, and then they hear a voice call something out.

The woman stands back up as people in the crowd nod their heads. She leaves the dias and crosses to an open part of the lawn that all of the other townsfolk have left clear. Then a second person walks up and sits on the throne.

"We've got to get closer," Doctor Zhao whispers.

"What are they doing?" Mara asks.

The wall they are peeking over curves around in a broad semicircle, encompassing the lawn and running into the mountains on either side of the dias.

"Let's go stand at the back of the crowd," Doctor Zhao says and climbs over the wall.

"Okay." Mara pulls herself up and drops over onto the grass.

"Hopefully no one sees us. Just act casual." Doctor Zhao whispers.

Mara nods. She puts her hands in her pockets and they stroll across the open grass, no big deal, just two peasants arriving a little late, that's all.

They make their way to the back of the crowd without being noticed. Doctor Zhao gives Mara a wink. She opens her eyes real wide and shrugs.

Another person walks up onto the dais and takes the throne.

"They all look alike," Mara says again under her breath. The people are washed with layers of dirt into a muddy medieval bedraggle.

The voice calls out again. "PEASANT." Now they can clearly hear that the voice is a recorded voice that has the buzzing tinniness of an old speaker.

"Doctor Zhao?" Mara whispers.

"Oh boy," Doctor Zhao chuckles.

"What?"

"It's the Party Throne," he whispers back. "Just watch."

Another person takes the throne. "PEASANT," the voice announces again.

"What's the Party Throne?" Mara asks, but then she remembers the map. "Wait, are we in the Party Kingdom?"

Doctor Zhao shrugs, "Perhaps so?"

The people in front of them glance back like annoyed people in a movie theater.

Doctor Zhao signals for Mara to watch.

"PEASANT," the throne announces again.

Another person sits on it.

"PEASANT."

Another person.

"PEASANT." Again!

But then something different,

"ROYAL GUARD." The woman sitting on the throne gives a satisfied sneer and hops up.

But then back to,

"PEASANT."

Mara sighs.

The throne continues to announce its way through the denizens of the kingdom. Almost everyone is assigned the role of peasant, but a few are merchants, like the tanner and the smith, and some are guards, and there's a pair of advisers and several servants of the court.

Mara and Doctor Zhao both gasp when the next person steps up to the throne.

It's Sarah!

Mara almost shouts her name, but Doctor Zhao whispers, "Wait until after."

Mara nods. She stands on her tiptoes to see Sarah better.

The recorded voice calls out, "PEASANT."

Sarah rolls her eyes, then gets up and joins the group near the gate.

Then Kreak hops onto the Dais.

"I'm glad we've found them!" Doctor Zhao whispers. Mara bounces on her toes in excitement.

"PEASANT."

Kreak grins and trots off the dais with a little skip.

"Uh oh," Doctor Zhao says.

The next person to walk up on the stage is the massive invader Carl.

"Oh, that guy," Mara groans.

"Yes. That guy tied me up and buried me in pillows."

"That guy threw Chawz at Kreak."

Carl sits on the throne. He's too big to fit in the seat, so he actually spans the arms. Pumping his fists, he says, "Come on, Come on..."

"PEASANT," the throne calls.

"Phooey!" Carl says and stomps down off the dais. He just makes it to the group near the gate when the next announcement happens.

"KING."

Carl throws up his arms, spins around and roars in shock. "Noo...Come on! By One!" he yells. "One! Missed me by one!"

"BOOOOOOO! BOOOO!" the crowd yells. Carl, as if he's been booed before, immediately slumps like a splashed cat and mopes back to the lawn.

"We need to go!" Mara whispers, noticing that they're aren't that many townsfolk left.

Doctor Zhao grabs her sleeve. "It's too late to leave."

There's just a handful of people standing in front of them now, the rest are all near the gate, watching.

"We're gonna be the last two people," Mara whispers.

"Um… oh boy," Doctor Zhao says. "Let's see what happens. I'll go first."

When it's finally just them, he walks up onto the dais and sits upon the throne.

As soon as they see him, Kreak and Sarah start waving. Doctor Zhao gives them a flick of his eyebrows.

"ROYAL GUARD."

"Hmm," Doctor Zhao says, then stands up. He scans the dais as he steps away from the throne.

"HEEYYYYYY YOUUUUU!" Carl emerges upwards through the crowd.

"BOOOOO! BOOO!" The crowd drowns his shouts out.

The giant grimaces and hunkers back down.

Mara, the very last person, makes her way onto the dais and sits upon the throne. Kreak and Sarah wave at her and Mara grins back.

"PEASANT."

Mara guesses she should have expected that.

She rushes over to her friends. "Sarah!" Mara jumps into Sarah's arms. "I was so worried about you guys."

"I was worried about you guys too!" Sarah says.

Kreak claps and says, "Marrraaa!" He bounces next to them with a big smile.

Around them though, the crowd of villagers is moving all at once. Peasants slug out the gates to work. The newly appointed Royal Guards huff up to the dias and don their arms from the pile where the last set of guards left them.

Doctor Zhao tells his friends, "Come back and wait for me by the wall once everyone settles into their new roles." He winks at Kreak and Sarah. "I'm glad we found you two." Then he heads up to find some armor that fits.

Sarah, Kreak and Mara follow the rest of the peasants.

"You ended up here too!" Mara says.

"Ya!" Kreak grins from ear to ear.

Sarah nods, then shakes her head, "Ya, but we don't know where here is, and these people are so strange!"

Mara glances back towards Doctor Zhao. On the dais, the new King, crowned and enrobed, picks up the scepter, and with a huge sneer, she takes her seat on the throne.

"Eww..." Mara says. "So where's everyone going now?"

"Peasant. We are Peasant." Kreak slaps his chest.

Sarah hooks Mara's elbow and explains what they've learned so far. "Peasants either work in the fields or find something to deliver or repair, anything really. But to be honest, between you and me, it seems like nothing actually gets done. Kreak's been helping me repair the wagon, no one here can fix it, they've forgotten how to make a wheel. Can you believe that? These people! They barely survive! The King! The King! I don't care who gets the role, they always want to build some statue or tomb, or tear one down, or dancing, Kings like to watch a lot of dancing, or sleeping, that too. And then the bell rings and we all get new roles. It's absurd. I've only ever been a Peasant."

"Kreak Peasant too." Kreak says.

"Ya same with Kreak," Sarah nods. "Carl was a guard once. He really enjoyed that, but he's crazy to be the King. You saw the way he acted before. He gets booed almost every time."

"Where is he?" Mara asks.

"Probably the fields. He actually makes a big difference out there." Then she laughs. "I guess Carl makes a big difference anywhere he goes."

Mara giggles.

"But he's really good with the plow. I think he even likes it, he's certainly very appreciated out there."

Mara stops them in the middle of the marketplace. Everyone here is just going about their business mindlessly. No one takes note of them at all. "These people don't even seem to see us."

Sarah throws her hand up. "This place! I'm telling you, something's wrong with them. It's like they're following a script. Peasants will only talk about Peasant things, no matter what you try. For example:

Me: 'Why do we change roles every hour?

Them: 'Not sure - Hey, have you seen how big that pig has gotten?

Or:

Me: 'Is there any way to leave this valley?

Them: 'Never looked – So you think that woodchuck I caught will taste good? Never ate a woodchuck yet.'

"So... Ya, those are the conversations I've been having." She hugs Mara again. "It's so good to finally have a normal one with someone other than Carl!"

"Hey! We conversator!" Kreak yells.

"Oh yes, you and I have excellent conversations." Sarah rubs his shoulder. He grins.

"The mountains are so tall!" Mara says. "Is there any way out? The bad guys want us to find a key. You guys can help us! But how did you get here?"

"Let's head back towards the court," Sarah says and leads them back. "A key? That sounds interesting. You know, I'm not sure how we got here. After you and Chawz disappeared, we got lost in the house, and then we fell down this crazy slide and landed in the top of an Oak tree out beyond the fields. Near the mountains."

"Auntie's house is so amazing. So many surprises," Mara says.

"Ya," Sarah nods.

"And slides. Lots of slides. I never could have imagined this place. Sarah, do you really think I'm good at..." Mara starts, but just then, Carl leers at them from behind a skewered varmint vendor's stand to their right.

"Hey there Mara," Carl sneers. "So glad you and Doc could join us in this crazy kingdom."

"Hello Carl," Mara replies cautiously.

"Wait until I'm the King here!" Carl grabs one of the skewers he's cooking and points it at them. "Cause you're going straight to the Dungeon!" He laughs.

"Carl," Mara says to him as calmly as she can. "Carl, what if one of us is the king first?"

Carl grimaces.

"Carl, don't you think we should work together?" Mara asks him.

Carl turns around, grabs a new stick and begins skewering some more varmint to cook.

Sarah shakes her head. "Seriously? You're going to sulk?"

"Think about it," Mara says to his huge back.

The three leave Carl to cook his snacks.

"Apparently he didn't go to the fields today," Sarah says.

As they approach the stone wall surrounding the court, Mara steers them off to the right. "I have an idea," she says. She leads them along the wall, all the way to where it meets the mountain next to the dias.

Mara grabs a rock, one of the many that have fallen from the ill maintained wall. "Grab that big one Kreak, let's fix this wall."

"Great idea," Sarah says.

Mara wishes her art could be great ideas too. But her sketchbook is starting to feel like a silly toy. Auntie's house is actually a really amazing original idea. An original idea filled with original ideas. Mara's face slowly hardens as she rebuilds the wall.

After a few minutes, the king suddenly yells, "STEADY YOU NUMBSKULLS! NOW MOVE OVER THERE!"

"Holy moly," Sarah says.

The guards, sardined together with their hands over their heads, have created an unstable platform which the King is standing on. Her arms splay out and shoot in all directions as the tower totters.

She points across the lawn. "GO NOW!"

The group begins to quaver in that direction. The guards face in all which ways, some shuffle backwards, others sidestep; the spidery mass of armored bodies clangs against itself, sways to the left, then backwards, and finally it makes a little forward ground.

The King hollers, "STEADY YOU LOUTS! Just go

forward, ARGH! WHOAAA! It's okay, I got it... KEEP GOING! There. NO THERE!"

Small flocks of pigeons are unsure which way to flee.

"This is crazy!" Mara says. "Can you tell which one is Doctor Zhao?"

"No way," Sarah says. "So crazy."

The gangle of guards teeter around the lawn at the King's whim.

After a ridiculous half an hour, the King now has the whole group almost at a run, moving straight towards the throne. "FASTER! FASTER! WhoaAA!! YA! Wait... WHOA! THE DAIS!"

"They're gonna run into it," Sarah says.

"TURN! TURN NOW! TUURRNN!" the King yells.

The Guards turn all at once. Some turn left. Some turn right. Others turn over. Clang! Blang! Bong! The King crashes down. Armor clatters. People yell. Arms and legs are so confused.

"Holy moly," Sarah gasps.

Mara blinks a few times. "Wow," she says.

The dust settles.

For quite some time.

Eventually, the King drags herself up the dais, onto the throne and begins eating. Most of the guards just lay still. A few of them jerk and shake themselves to their feet.

One of the guards gets up and shambles indirectly across the lawn towards Mara, Kreak and Sarah.

"Doctor Zhao! Are you okay?" Mara asks.

Doctor Zhao leans against the wall for a few minutes, heaving.

He gasps out, "She thought it looked fun when they carried us, when the guards carried you and I out of here before. She thought it looked fun..."

"Looked fun!" Kreak proclaims.

"Yes, well, maybe for her, but I tell you, being sandwiched in the middle of a group of people... Not knowing which way to go... Being stepped on... She was stomping on us to go faster! This was not a pleasurable experience." Doctor Zhao stretches his arms up, then puts them on his hips and bends backwards a bit. "Eeeeya," he groans. "Errf." He does some head circles, "I did ask some of the other guards about a way out of the valley, but no luck."

"Well what are we gonna do?" Sarah asks.

"I think we can use the throne to change the game here."

"How?" Mara asks.

Doctor Zhao glances over his shoulder—the rest of the court is still mostly comatose after the King's people-mobile adventure.

"Why don't they care about us?" Mara asks. "We look different, we're dressed different."

"They're totally oblivious." Doctor Zhao turns back to his friends. "They're so caught in the game, they don't even know they're playing it. And actually, we don't look that different." He waves his hand at their clothing.

Mara checks herself out. "Oh boy..."

Her overalls are a complete mess. The tatters and tears from the ocean and Globe Island are encrusted with grime and mud from their slide through the mountain. The quick dip in these people's sacred well barely made a dent in the layers of dirt. Kreak and Sarah are just as bedraggled. "Mmm, we fit right in I guess," Mara says.

Doctor Zhao raises his finger. "Yes, but even so, these people have switched off their critical thinking."

"Can we switch it back on?" Mara asks.

"I think so," Doctor Zhao nods. Then he leans in close. "I manage the inventory for these warehouses that are full of things your Aunt designed. When your aunt created this house, a lot of random objects from the warehouses ended up inside of it. The Party Throne is one of those objects and, well, I've actually read the description about it."

"Awesome," Sarah says.

"You read the instructions?" Mara asks.

"For the throne, yes. It's a stroke of luck! I remember that there's a control panel on the back of it."

"Can you turn it off?" Sarah asks.

"Most certainly," Doctor Zhao nods.

"Can you change what it says?" Mara asks.

"Yes, that's what I was thinking also," Doctor Zhao nods again. "But what would we have it say?"

"How's it work?" Sarah puts in.

"Well, it's a party game really. The Party Throne assigns roles to people and they play out those roles for a bit, then the bell rings, and they get new roles. It's for fun, a type of theater game."

"But...where'd these people come from?" Mara pulls herself up a little higher. The guards are back on their feet doing drills for the King, drills they have no clue how to do. They're in danger of skewering each other. "Geez."

Doctor Zhao shakes his head. "I have no idea where these people came from to be honest, but somehow the house is just full of different kinds of people."

"If one of us were the King we could order the people to show us the way, or at least to answer our questions," Sarah says.

"Yes! King! Peasant!" Kreak shouts.

"Mmm, I don't think I can pinpoint one of us to be the King," Doctor Zhao says.

But up on the dais, the current King hears Kreak shout. "YOUUU! GUARD! YOUU! GET OVER HERE!"

Doctor Zhao looks back at the King. His gulp is audible.

"YA! YOU! GET OVER HERE, LAZY VARMINT!"

"Doctor Zhao, what are we going to do?" Mara blurts out as he turns.

"I have an idea!" he shout-whispers back.

"Um… Okay..." Mara says as he runs off.

The King waves away all the other guards. Then she solo drills Doctor Zhao. "UP! DOWN! LOWER WEAPON!

FORWARD! DOWN! RAISE WEAPON!...”

“Geez,” Sarah says. “She hasn’t lost her voice at all. Poor Doctor Zhao.”

Doctor Zhao plays the king’s exhausting game of invisible piñata, while Mara, Sarah and Kreak continue to replace the wall’s fallen stones.

“Well at least this wall is looking better.” Mara wipes her hair back.

From the closest market stall, the fishmonger holds up a fish and salutes. “Hard work for the King! Huzzah!”

“Huzzah!” Mara and Sarah reply.

Finally The King yells, “Enough!” And with a wave of her hand, dismisses Doctor Zhao.

Doctor Zhao can barely lift his spear and seems to have actually shrunken a bit. He slowly drags himself to the dais and joins the other guards who are scattered around. The King turns to her plate of food and tosses gristle to the mangy dogs who scrap near the throne.

Mara glances up from time to time, but Doctor Zhao’s splayed flat out on the dias like spilt milk.

After just a bit longer, the bell chimes the changing of the roles. “Bng-BOng BONG, B-bong-bn, BOONGH, BnBONG BONG!”

Automatically, the townsfolk drop what they’re doing, mid-stride, mid-sentence, mid-scoop, and they head to the field in front of the throne.

Mara and her friends join the lot.

Up on the dais, Doctor Zhao lifts his helmeted head a bit and groans, but then his head falls back to the ground. Clang! "Oof! Ow!" He sits up, sways a bit, then he crawls towards the back of the throne.

Mara whispers to Sarah, "Look, Doctor Zhao is doing something."

Sarah replies, "Oh ya."

As they watch Doctor Zhao, Mara says, "These people are barely getting by, did you see the food in the market?"

"The apples are actually pretty good, but everything looks just horrible," Sarah whispers back.

"And their homes are falling apart."

"The whole kingdom is a total mess."

"And the King is so mean again."

"Right?" Sarah rolls her eyes.

"I hope Doctor Zhao fixes this."

As the crowd settles on the grass in front of the throne, Doctor Zhao stumbles over to his friends.

"Are you okay Doctor Zhao?" Mara asks.

Barely able to keep himself on his feet, he whispers, "I did it."

"What did you do?" Mara and Sarah both ask at the same time.

They grin at their jinx.

"You'll see. You'll see," Doctor Zhao gasps out.

But then he grimaces. "Oh no, Carl's trying to go first. Oh boy."

Carl plows out of the crowd onto the dais. He turns and throws up his fists, then he takes the throne.

The tinny recorded voice from within the throne speaks. "KING."

Carl jumps up. "YESSS! YESSS! I AM THE KING! YESSS!"

The crowd murmurs.

"Oh no," Mara says.

"Holy Moly," Sarah exclaims.

Carl rejoices his way over to the empty open area of the grass by the gate. "THE KING! YESS! FINALLY! FINALLY! YESSS!" He doesn't stop cheering for himself.

"BOOOO!" The crowd yells, and fortunately, like a trained pony, Carl shrinks and quiets down.

"Thank goodness," Sarah says.

Once the crowd settles, another person steps up and takes the throne.

The metallic voice announces, "KING."

Total silence as the man stands up with a confused look.

Water drips into the sacred well.

Leaves whisper in the breeze.

Then Carl roars, "NOOOO! I AM THE KING! NOT YOU! ME! ME!"

"Oh boy..." Doctor Zhao says.

"BOOOOO! BOOO!" The crowd yells him down again, but people mutter and crow as the second King gives Carl a little space.

The crowd becomes totally quiet as the next person approaches the throne.

"KING."

Loud chatter now as heads bob and turn to each other.

"Doctor Zhao?" Mara whispers.

"This will work," he says. "Everyone will be King and then we'll have to talk to each other and figure out what to do."

"Doctor Zhao, I don't want to be King," Sarah says.

"Everyone will be equal," Doctor Zhao says. "What could go wrong?"

One by one, up to the throne. One by one, the word, once so powerful, weakens with repetition.

"King."

"King."

"King."

Until everyone, Mara and her friends included, the whole lot, everyone is King. They all stand together in the grass by the gate, looking at each other for a few moments.

Then a popcorn spatter of voices declare, "I am the King." Then louder, more voices, shouting now. Then a rumble passes through the crowd.

Kreak grabs the two girls, and with an extra finger, hooks Doctor Zhao also, then he leaps them out of the way as the whole crowd suddenly rushes towards the throne.

"Holy Moly!" Sarah cries out as the stampede of screaming people fly past. Carl leads the rampage with two other Kings held high over his head. "I AM THE KING! I AM THE KING!" everyone yells.

"Oh no," Doctor Zhao says.

"Doctor Zhao…" Mara whispers.

Dust surges from the stampede and rises up in front of them.

They four of them lie there in a billowy blurred shock.

Eventually Kreak helps everyone to their feet as the cloud disperses.

"Holy Moly!" Sarah cries out.

A gigantic ball of humanity is congealed to the throne. It covers most of the dais, and almost touches the rocky overhang above. Legs, stomachs, heads, everything, the entire population is struggling to sit on the throne. People sandwich, stretch and contort, they even squeeze between each other, to place a single finger or toe on the throne.

"Woah." Mara says.

After a few minutes of shock, Sarah mutters, "Holy moly moly moly."

Doctor Zhao takes a deep breath. "Oh boy."

Mara takes a few steps towards forward and then looks back at her friends, "Can we change this?"

Sarah joins her. "Somehow? Right away?"

"Yes. Yes we can," Doctor Zhao nods. As the group approaches the dais he says, "If I can get to the back of the throne, I can make the bell go again. I could set it so everyone's a... maybe a baker? How about that?"

Sarah shakes her head. "I don't know Doctor Zhao, these people will just fight over the oven or the rolling pin."

"Can you make it say whatever you want?" Mara asks.

"I think so," Doctor Zhao says. "Do you have an idea?"

"Well, we need them to talk to us."

Sarah jumps in, "Auntie told me once about inspirational speakers. She said they're a little funny but most of them do a lot of good for the world."

"A whole kingdom full of Inspirational Speakers?" Doctor Zhao says. "That would be something."

"But we need them to listen too," Mara says.

Kreak's brow furrows deeply. "Hmmmmmm."

"What about artists?" Doctor Zhao puts out.

Mara shrugs, "I love art, but..."

Kreak says, "Tribe." He bobs.

"Tribe," Mara repeats. "Tribe member... citizen. Hey, what about citizen?"

"Now that sounds perfect," Doctor Zhao says. "Citizenship typically means being free to work, live and have a choice in the politics of a society."

"Let's do it!" Sarah claps her hands.

"Cideezin!" Kreak cries out.

"Good idea Kreak." Mara pats him. He is delighted.

The group moves closer to the dais.

The wavering mass of Kings slow fights for the throne. People strain. They struggle. They try to worm towards the center of the great human meatball.

Mara shakes her head. "Doctor Zhao, how are you going to...?"

Sarah cuts in, "There's like twenty feet of people you have to get through Doctor Zhao."

"The control panel is on the back, on the bottom. Maybe I could somehow tunnel underneath them?"

Sarah throws up a finger. "Wait, I have an idea." She runs out into the grass a little ways, then turns back, "Hey!" she yells really loud. "Hey! Festival for the King! The King is needed! The King! It's a festival for the King on the far side of the fields! The King needs to be there!"

The meatball pauses. Then it spasms and writhes. Then it urchins until people pop out.

"Back!" Doctor Zhao shouts, and they all leap back.

With a burble and a burp, the meatball collapses. Humans by the bundle, puddle across the dais, and then with a boil, they scramble to their feet.

Talking all at once, they scurry towards the fields. "The King is needed." "I must go!" "A festival for me, how nice." "Make way!" "Make way for the King!" Talking on top of each other, the kings elbow and shove past each other. Carl, who formed

137

the core of the meatball, is among the last to get to his feet.

"Where's everyone going?" he yells.

Sarah points. "The festival for the King. It's in the fields."

"I am the King!" Carl bellows.

"You should get over there," Sarah says.

"Yes. Yes I should." Carl puffs out his chest and sets off.

As soon as he's gone, Doctor Zhao says, "OK let's do this."

On the back of the throne, just above the short lion-footed-legs, a door blends into the paneling.

Doctor Zhao reaches underneath the seat and flips a switch. The door pops open to reveal a small screen and a keyboard. Doctor Zhao removes KING from the list of active roles, and he types in CITIZEN. He sets the quantity to UNLIMITED, and then he arranges for the bell to ring only one time without any repetition. He confirms his entries, closes the panel door and stands.

The bell rings right away, "BLONG-BbONG!! bon-BONGS obong-bBONG! Bng..."

"They're coming back already," Mara says.

She and her friends head down to the grass.

The townsfolk return through the gate, automated again by the call of the throne, but this time, their movements are a little more jerky and agitated.

"Carl looks disappointed." Sarah says, making Mara giggle.

After everyone arrives, a woman walks onto the dais and sits on the throne. The speaker scratches and then the tinny voice says, "CITIZEN."

The word hangs in the air. The woman sits there for a moment. The word swirls and spirals its way around her, until she remembers. Citizen. Then the woman gives an actual real smile. She stands, and lightly steps her way over to the open area of the lawn.

One after another the townsfolk take the throne.

"CITIZEN." "CITIZEN." So different! "CITIZEN." Some laughter. Eye contact. "CITIZEN." Heads nod. "CITIZEN." Wonder! "CITIZEN."

After all are given the role of citizen, everyone just stands around for a few minutes. Thinking.

Then they begin to talk. Conversations spark with a quiet clatter of questions. There's a trickle of responses. The tide of interaction rises higher. Salt cliffs of ideas melt away before thunderous storms of discussion. "How do we live?" "How do we make choices?"

Mara and her friends listen to the crowd.

Agreements overrule arguments and then crash into conflicting opinions, carrying the conversation forward.

"Shall we?" Doctor Zhao says to his companions, and then leads the way over.

The people welcome them.

"They're introducing themselves," Mara whispers to Sarah.

"It's great, right?" Sarah whispers back.

"So, what's going on here?" Doctor Zhao asks a man

named Jehosephat.

"We're figuring that out!" Jehosephat laughs. "We're all citizens now, so we all get to decide things, make choices, and figure out how we want to live."

"As a group," his wife Bridgette adds.

"That's just great," Doctor Zhao says

Jehosephat nods enthusiastically. "We want everyone to have an equal say. We have agreed on one choice already."

"What's that?" Mara asks.

"We're calling ourselves a 'Cooperation,'" Jehosephat says with a grin.

"My my my. Simply fantastic," Doctor Zhao says and pats Kreak on the back. Then he leans in and whispers to his friends. "Why don't we get rid of that throne for them, ya?"

"Yes please," Sarah says. "But you guys go ahead, I'm gonna see if anyone knows a way out of the valley."

"Good idea," Mara says, then her and Kreak and Doctor Zhao slip away, up to the throne.

Once they're standing by it, Mara asks, "It's really a very pretty throne. Where do we put it?"

Doctor Zhao shrugs, "Hide it somewhere? Bury it?"

"Smash?" Kreak bobs.

"It's a piece of art!" Mara says.

"Ehh, it's a good game also Kreak," Doctor Zhao adds.

Mara gives a sneaky smile and says, "What about a label that says, 'For Entertainment Purposes Only'?"

140

"That might work," Doctor Zhao chuckles. "Silly."

Mara giggles.

They examine the throne and they soon discover latches that lock the legs into place. Flipping the latches, they rotate the throne a few degrees, then pull it free from the leg sockets.

After setting it back down to the side, Mara says, "Maybe there's a store room somewhere?"

But just then Carl walks up. "Is it going to bong again?" Carl asks.

"No," Doctor Zhao answers.

"Good," Carl says. He glances over his shoulder at the townsfolk. "Do you think they will let me stay and join their Cooperation?"

"Yes," Mara nods at him with a smile, "Yes, I'm sure they'd love to have you."

"You sure?" Carl asks.

"But you're gonna have to help everyone, not just... um...serve yourself. And you have to help make choices too."

"I want that," he says. "I'm sick of being told what to do. But... I don't wanna give orders either." He shrugs his massive shoulders. "I'm sick of it."

Doctor Zhao wags his finger. "Carl, not too long ago you were kidnapping people and throwing your friends at them."

"I know," Carl says, hanging his head down for a moment. "I'm sorry about that. But lemme tell you, I got to be the King, I got to do that and you know what? I didn't like being in the center of all those people. It was horrible."

"I'll bet," Sarah says.

"I realized, I just want to see Chawz, and I want to see more of this house." He looks up at the mountains for a moment. "Ya know, I feel different since coming here. There're things." He shakes his head. "Well, I don't wanna be at odds with The Designer anymore, that's all I'm sayin'. Maybe I could ask her, maybe I could live here, ya know, here in her world."

Mara says, "Carl we need to save Auntie first! From your boss. We need to find some key to some vault so The Lady Banks doesn't... so she doesn't hurt Auntie. We need to get out of the valley. We need to..." Getting upset, she turns away and crosses her arms tightly.

"She's really your aunt then, eh?" Carl asks.

"Yes she is," Mara says.

Then Carl kneels down and holds out one hand to her, and the other to Kreak, and says, "For what it's worth, I'm sorry I captured you both. You big guy, I'm sorry I threw Chawz at you. I hopes you all can forgive me."

Mara looks over her shoulder, then turns back around and takes Carl's huge hand in her own and shakes it. "All right, I forgive you."

Kreak gapes at Carl's huge hand in his own. "You big guy," he says.

"Big parents," Carl nods.

Kreak looks up at him, "I forgive."

Carl stands back up. "Thank you. You'll see. Hey do you know where Chawz is?"

"I do," Mara says. "He's with this really cool teacher, Seergart, and he's learning about his sacred tone."

"That sounds pretty neat," Carl says.

"After we help Auntie, then maybe Doctor Zhao can take you to him?" Mara looks up at Doctor Zhao.

"I certainly can," Doctor Zhao nods. "But first we need to get out of this valley. Carl, you don't by chance happen to know a way out?"

"Nope," Carl shakes his head. "But maybe that map shows the way." He points down at his feet where the throne once stood.

"What map?" Mara asks.

"That one right there." Carl points again at the floor by his feet.

Mara moves next to him and stands directly over the spot Carl is pointing at. "Oh wow! Doctor Zhao look."

Doctor Zhao leans in. "My goodness, the engraving is so fine that the map is only visible from directly above. I think if Carl wasn't so tall, we might have missed it completely." He glances up at the giant. "Thank you Carl!"

Carl gives a big thumbs up.

"This would have been impossible to see with the throne in place," Doctor Zhao adds. "Quite well hidden."

The map traces the circular valley. They see that from the dais at one end, the little town radiates out to fields and forest which stretch to the mountains on the far side. All the way across from the dais, far from any other structure, the map shows a staircase that climbs all the way up the mountains.

"Hah!" Doctor Zhao puts his finger on it. "Looks like we found our exit."

Doctor Zhao kneels and leans close to the map. "There's a word written by the stairs." He rubs his eyes. "I think your eyes might be better than mine Mara, can you read this?"

Mara gets down on her belly. The tiny scrawl squiggles into letters as she closes in. "I can barely read it. Nabu? Nabu. I think it says Nabu."

Doctor Zhao stands up and throws his hands up. "Of course! We need to find Nabu!" He dances around in a circle.

"What's Nabu?" Mara stands up.

"Who is Nabu, you mean." He shakes and pumps his fists back and forth. Then he settles back down and smoothes his lapel. "I should have thought of him earlier, he knows everything. Nabu's a super computer guy. Totally connected."

"Well let's go find him," Mara says.

Mara looks down at the map one last time. But when she compares it to her own drawing skills, she frowns. She could never draw something that beautiful. Mara taps her sketchbook. Maybe she's not really an artist at all. She doesn't think she'd ever be able to make lines that graceful. Maybe she really is just Miss Scribbles.

Doctor Zhao gives a big clap of his hands. "Yes, let's find

Nabu."

Mara walks towards the edge of the dais, looking out at the former kingdom. Auntie designed all of this. Mara's face twitches.

"What about the throne?" Carl asks.

"Hmm..." Doctor Zhao scratches his chin.

"I have an idea." The giant says and picks up the throne like it's a child's stool. Then he tosses it over his shoulder into the sacred well.

"All gone." He wipes the dust off his hands.

Doctor Zhao laughs, "Well that works."

The throne sinks to the bottom.

Carl bows, "Okay, I'm gonna go join the Cooperation. Thank you guys for being so nice." Carl bows at them again, then lopes off the dais.

Just then, Sarah runs up and joins them. "What's up with the big guy? Mara, what's wrong?"

"Nothing." Mara shakes her head, and tries to smile. "Carl turned good," she says. "Oh, and we found a map!"

"That's great!" Sarah says, but she can tell something is wrong with Mara.

The group watches Carl join the Cooperation, where great discussion and conversation is happening. Then Mara sighs and says, "Let's go guys." And she walks off the dais.

Sarah gives Doctor Zhao a look, but he shrugs his shoulders.

They catch up with Mara, and the group heads across the

valley towards the stairs.

Chapter 12: Ascent

With the map of the valley in their minds, Mara and her friends left the citizens of the valley to decide their own future and they traveled over the lawn, past the market, across the fields, into the woods, and all the way to the mountains on the far side of the valley. But after spending what must have been at least an hour searching the cliff face, Sarah throws up her arms. "There's no staircase!"

The white veined, grey stone mountain rises vertically in front of them, insurmountable and intimidating.

"According to that map, it should be right here," Doctor Zhao says.

Sarah puts her hands on her hips and huffs. "We've searched the whole side."

Mara runs her hands over the steep wall of stone once again. She hasn't said much at all, but now she grumbles, "It goes almost straight up. I think we're gonna have to go back."

Sarah joins her. "One last sweep," she says.

"Fine." Mara says.

They feel over the surface of the mountain again, moving in opposite directions to explore the surface.

This time though, after just a moment, Doctor Zhao shouts out, "Sarah, your arm just shot forward."

"Oh, it's just a shift in the wall here."

"But it looks flat to me. Can you run back over that spot?" He moves sideways to get a better angle. Mara trudges over.

"Hey!" Sarah exclaims. "You're right, this is kinda weird. Look." Sarah sticks her arm straight into the mountain.

"How'd you do that?" Mara says.

"Move around behind me." Sarah flicks her head.

"My, my, my..." Doctor Zhao mutters. Sarah steps aside for him and he reaches forward to touch the mountain. But he just keeps going until he loses his balance, windmills half-way, but then he lands awkwardly, at an upward angle. "Oof! That didn't hurt!"

"It looks like you're laying on the mountain," Mara says.

"It's the stairs!" he cries out. "I'm leaning on the stairs." Doctor Zhao feels around beneath him. "Yup, these are definitely the stairs." Then pushes himself up. "Amazing. This staircase is a masterwork in deception. We'd never have found this just by looking."

Mara feels the first stair with her hands, then steps up past Doctor Zhao. "You can see em better when you're standing on em."

Sarah also reaches out with her hands first, then she climbs up to Mara. "This house is crazy!"

Mara thinks it's the most amazing, most creative house in

the whole world. Sarah hasn't even seen Doctor Zhao's map. Mara's been trying to design a house in her head, but she keeps crushing it into little pieces and starting over. In her mind, she slams a hammer down on the boring log cabin she was working on. She figures she might as well just let the dark cloud that's filling her head do it's thing.

Sarah waves down to Kreak. "Come on Kreak."

But Kreak is crouching by a boulder, swaying back and forth with a look of horror on his face.

"It's okay Kreak." Sarah runs back down. "Do you want to hold my hand?"

"Ya," he nods.

They take the first few steps really slow. "See, you can do it," Sarah says.

"Keep hold hand."

"I will."

They pass Doctor Zhao, who follows. Mara's already trudging ahead. The group heads up the hidden stairway, switching their way back and forth across the surface of the mountain. Fairly quickly actually, they rise above the trees and the fields, and soon the town across the valley comes into view.

Mara lets Sarah and Kreak pass her so she can walk with Doctor Zhao, but she doesn't say anything.

After a moment, he gently asks her, "Mara, what's wrong?"

Her face gets really hard, and she pushes her lips tight. She tries to keep a hold of the dark cloud in her mind. But then her breathing stutters a few times, and tears swell in her eyes. She presses them closed hard. But some tears escape and slide down her cheeks.

She looks up at Doctor Zhao, then sobs out, "Doctor Zhao will you please not tell Auntie about my talent." Her sobs wrench her words, she wipes at her nose. "I've decided that I'm not going to show her my sketchbooks."

"Oh Mara…"

"No!" She cries. "I've made up my mind. I'm not a good artist. I'll never be a good artist. And once we save Auntie, I just want to go back to school and be normal. I'll be a doctor or something like my parents want."

"Mara, you are a very talented artist."

"No I'm not!" she says. She swipes at her face with her sleeves. Her breathing is loud and ragged.

Sarah runs back down the stairs and grabs Mara into a huge hug and squeezes her back and forth. "It's okay sister, you can cry if you want."

Mara crumbles into Sarah's shoulder and lets herself cry.

"There you go sister, there you go." Sarah cradles her tight.

Kreak, who made his way carefully back down, grabs onto Doctor Zhao's coat. "Marraaa?"

"She'll be okay," Doctor Zhao whispers to him.

Mara cries until the dark cloud has no power, and her invincible summer can't help but shine again.

Her breathing finally steadies, and Sarah holds her out.

"Got it out?"

"Ya." A last few after-sobs shake her. Then Mara wipes her face clean with her sleeves and sniffs her nose. She half-smiles up at Sarah. "Thank you," she says.

"Shall we go save Auntie?" Sarah asks.

"Ya." Mara nods.

"Good." Sarah squeezes Mara's shoulders then lets her go. She steps back up to Kreak and takes his hand again.

"Mara…" Doctor Zhao starts.

But Mara interrupts, "I know you have to tell Auntie about my talent. But I'm not going to show her my drawings."

"Well, I guess what I was thinking," Doctor Zhao says. "Is that Auntie will know just what to say to you Mara. I'm sure of it."

"Hmm." Mara glances up at Doctor Zhao.

"I'm sure of it," he says again.

Mara looks down at her feet. "Auntie always knows what to say." Then she looks back up at Doctor Zhao and musters a little smile. "Let's go save her."

He winks. "Let's go save her."

When they catch up with Sarah and Kreak, Sarah points up the stairs and says, "Have you guys noticed how far we've gone already? We're like almost to the top of the mountain. But look down, we aren't even that high. Doctor Zhao, what's going on here?" She puts her hands on her hips again, looking up, then down.

Doctor Zhao says, "I think it's part of the mountain's trick.

It's deceiving us again, just like the stairs. Come on, let's keep going."

So they continue climbing.

Mara goes ahead and takes Kreak's other hand, because he's definitely not enjoying this at all. He's just staring straight down at the stairs and refuses to look up.

"Almost there," Mara says to him.

And after just a few more switchbacks, they walk up to the sky.

Doctor Zhao laughs and touches the sky. "Painted," he says. "We're still inside. I was wondering about that. Look, from here, you can clearly see the curve of the wall overhead."

"Wow," Mara says.

Her and Sarah both touch the painted sky, even Kreak runs his hands over the wall. "Ooooo."

Doctor Zhao takes a few steps back and looks up. "This house never ceases to amaze me."

"But why do the mountains seem so tall?" Sarah asks.

"Trompe L'oeil," Doctor Zhao chuckles. "It's a french term that means 'trick of the eye.' The mountains are designed to appear much taller than they are. The lines and angles soar away from the observer, making everything seem larger and more daunting."

"But the woods look pretty close from up here, which kinda breaks up the illusion," Mara says.

"Yes." Doctor Zhao agrees. "Oh look! A door." He points it out in the painted sky off to their left a little ways, and they move over to it.

"The doorknob kinda gives it away," Sarah says.

Mara nods, "Ya, what were they thinking?"

Sarah laughs with her.

Doctor Zhao rolls his eyes at them, then he opens the door and they peek in.

Kreak instantly leaps back with a yell, "Aaaaaaaaahhh!"

Chapter 13: Industry

The door in the sky at the top of the mountain opens wide. The whole group stumbles back as Kreak leaps away in horror.

Mara glances through the door. Then she giggles and reaches out to Kreak. "Kreak! It's okay!" She grabs his hand. "It's a mirror. Come look"

Sarah laughs and Doctor Zhao grins.

"Me roar?" Kreak slowly moves towards the door holding Mara's hand. He peeks in, but leaps right back again. "Who that?" he cries out, pointing.

"It's us Kreak. It's a reflection. Come on, I'll show you." Mara drags him forward. "Come on Kreak!"

Mara leads him through the door in the sky, and Doctor Zhao and Sarah follow them into the small square room.

The whole wall across from the door is covered by an old lead-backed mirror. It's veined and spotted, but clear enough.

"See, it's us." Mara touches the mirror. "This is a mirror."

Kreak's eyes get really big. "Mirroar." He moves back and forth gaping at his reflection.

"Look how dirty we are," Sarah says. "We're covered in grime from head to toe."

Mara starts to pick the pieces of straw and plant parts from her mud encrusted hair. "Eww."

Kreak moves his arm up and down. "Me," he says, and steps slowly side to side as he approaches the mirror. He touches his face. Then he waves his foot in the air.

"Um, Doctor Zhao, "Mara says. "This room doesn't have another door."

Sarah looks around and groans, "Great. This house is one puzzle after another!"

Doctor Zhao backs away from the mirror and surveys the room, "We can solve it. There's got to be a way forward."

The small room's empty except for a steam trunk, and a dusty old wooden spinning wheel in one of the corners.

Sarah goes over to check it out. "This looks broken." She tries to turn the wheel, but the gears slip and stall. "It's got eight spools on it, you could make a lot of thread with this thing." Then she shifts her attention to the steam trunk. "Let's see what's in here."

Mara and Doctor Zhao search the rest of the room while Sarah digs through the trunk. "It's full of wooden parts and cotton," she says. "We could fix the wheel and make some string," she snorts and closes the trunk.

"Actually I think that's what we need to do," Doctor Zhao replies. "Look up there, and there." He points up to the corners of the roof above either side of the mirrored wall. In the dim light, they can see that there are pulleys hanging there attached to ropes

155

that lead up through holes in the ceiling.

Then he walks over and touches the very center of the mirror. "And here in the middle of this mirror is a seam, it's very hard to see."

Mara heads over to him. "Oh, I see it now," she says. "You think if we can turn those pulleys, this wall will open?"

"We might as well try. Let's make some rope and see."

They gather around the broken spinning wheel. It's very old looking, but somewhat complex. Unlike the simple spinning wheels that feed a single spool, this one has its wheel mounted horizontally on its side instead of upright.

"Look, it's got a name—Jenny." Mara points at the worn remnants of lettering on it's frame.

"Jenny needs some help, eh?" Doctor Zhao kneels down next to the old wooden machine. "Thankfully she has replaceable parts. Replaceable parts are what led to the industrial revolution."

A lot of Jenny's parts need replacing. Some of the spinning wheel's pieces have warped or cracked, and a few have been eaten up and abandoned by bugs long ago.

Sarah heaves the trunk closer to the old machine and flips it open.

First the group dusts Jenny off, and then, part by part, they puzzle her back into working condition again. The trunk has enough wooden dowels, gears, frame boards and spindles to build a whole nother wheel, so it doesn't take that long to get Jenny looking good as new.

Doctor Zhao gives the foot pedal a try. The gears catch smoothly, the rods pump up and down and all eight spindles spin like they should. "We did it!" he shouts.

Sarah cheers and pats Mara on the back. Kreak bobs and claps his hands with delight.

"Good work team!" Doctor Zhao says. "Now let's make some rope!"

So they get to work. Mara and Sarah feed cotton into Jenny's wheel, while Doctor Zhao pumps the foot pedal. The wheel spins the cotton into thread and Doctor Zhao nimbly guides the thread to the eight spools where the thread winds around and around.

"Don't get your hair caught." Sarah jokes.

Mara laughs with her. "I won't," she says.

As the cotton whips around the wheel and spins into thread, and the thread flies through the machine towards the spools, they all watch with excitement.

"This type of spinning wheel was one of the very first machines ever created." Doctor Zhao says. "One of the very first tools to use replaceable parts. It's invention signaled the dawn of the Industrial Age."

The movement of the machine is like watching the ocean, or staring into a fire, too fast for the eyes to focus, so the mind dreams. Mara's mind drifts, and dinosaurs wander through her thoughts. Cavemen with sticks and stones. Nomads farming. Sailing ships crossing oceans. Humans meeting humans for good or ill. Behind her visions, there is a beating, a rhythm, a pulse. Something that winds the story together into a single thread.

Soon enough the spools on the spinning Jenny are almost full. Mara looks up from the movement at her friends. There's something that connects them all. Something that makes Mara feel warm, something that makes her forget how unhappy she felt climbing up the mountain.

"This works really fast," she says. The wheel turns. The spools spin round and round, gathering in the thread and growing fat.

Finally the spools are full. Jenny's finished her work. Doctor Zhao stops pumping the foot pedal. They retrieve the eight spools of thread and the four of them move to the center of the room.

"I've made lots of rope," Sarah says. "My tribe, we'd always be making rope around the fire at night." She shows them how to fold the thread and roll it against their thighs, twisting the thread back onto itself.

They fold and twist and fold and twist, and their lines get thicker and thicker. After a bit of work, they soon have two nice long lengths of rope.

"Right so," Doctor Zhao says, testing the strength of the rope they've made. "Wow, very strong. Let's do this."

They weave the ropes into the two pulleys. Doctor Zhao and Sarah station themselves at one, with Mara and Kreak working on the other.

Once they get their ropes fed through the two pulleys, Doctor Zhao says, "Gently now." And they pull.

The two pulleys on either side of the room slowly turn. They hear crusted gears hidden in the ceiling grumble to life. A loud groan, ominous whines, Kreak cowers slightly, but the ropes keep turning the pulleys.

The groans gets louder until a spray of dust bursts from the seam in the mirrored wall. Poof! Then the wall splits away and slides open.

"Yay!" Sarah and Mara cheer. Doctor Zhao looks very pleased indeed.

The four of them walk into the second small chamber, which is exactly the same size as the first.

"Holy Moly!" Sarah says. "There's no door again!"

"Don't despair," Doctor Zhao says. "There's probably a door, we just have to figure it out."

The second room doesn't have a mirror, but there is a big engine on one side. Dark black iron tubes, tanks, and cogwheels. Doctor Zhao inspects this with Sarah and Kreak, while Mara takes a look at the rest of the room.

"There's lots of little holes in the ceiling, and a bunch in the walls too," Mara points out. "And there's a big drain in the floor, but the grate's fixed in place, not that we'd fit down it."

The wall across from where they entered is dark grey cement like the rest of the room. "Ya guys, there's a seam in the wall here, like before. The machine will probably open it, right?"

she says.

"I hope so." Doctor Zhao nods. "This steam engine's in fine shape. Shouldn't be too hard to get it running."

"Steam engines and spinning wheels?" Sarah holds up her hands.

"Spinning Jenny." Doctor Zhao winks.

"Okay, Spinning Jenny. A nice wooden door with hinges, maybe a doorknob, this would be nice. But no, here, instead, we have steam-engine powered doors."

"Oh come on, when was the last time you got to fix a steam engine?" Doctor Zhao slaps a wrench in her hands.

They tighten nuts and bolts, they oil gears and pistons, and they clean the pipes.

Finally, Doctor Zhao says, "Okay, I think we're good now. Let's see what happens."

Sarah turns the valve and the boiler fills with water. From a metal bin, Kreak shovels coal into the furnace.

"Add water and fire," Doctor Zhao intones as he lights the coal.

They stand back as the heat rises. Water boils and pressure builds. Rods move and the giant piston slides back and forth.

Sarah yells, "So noisy!"

"The door's gonna open any second," Mara says.

But the door doesn't open. A gurgling sound rises that seems to come from under the ground, from deep in the mountain itself. They huddle together as it gets louder and louder.

160

Then it begins to rain. It pours. Water floods through all the little holes in the roof and they get totally soaked. "Holy Moly!" Sarah yells.

They're drenched in a second. But the water is pleasantly warm, and after the initial deluge, the downpour becomes less of a torrent and more like an overzealous shower.

Mara closes her eyes and turns her face up to the water. Without thinking she begins drawing on her mind's sketchbook. A forest, quick and fast, trees form with each stroke. Without flipping to a new page she draws a city on top of the trees, bold dark lines, she smudges hard with her thumb, the billows from smoke stacks. She weaves two dark lines around the page and scratches a train onto them.

Chugga chugga, chugga chugga, CHOO CHOO! The steam pushes the pistons. The water from the ceiling tap tap taps against Mara's forehead.

Mara suddenly remembers that she's decided she's not going to be an artist. The unintentional little smile drops from her face, and in her thoughts, she steps back from her sketchbook. The sketchbook floats before her in her mind eye. Mara's face tightens. The drawing is horrible. She tears the page from the sketchbook and vaporizes it. Then she blows up her sketchbook.

Mara opens her eyes and stares through the water at the wall in front of her. She will make an excellent doctor.

In the room, a loud switch clicks, and the water from the ceiling slows to a dribble and then stops. The four of them wipe the water from their eyes. All the grime, dirt and dust that they've collected has been washed away.

But just as the last drops fall from the ceiling, hot air suddenly blasts out of the holes in the walls and blows them all into each other. Kreak's cheeks whip full of air and his tongue gets blown aside. "Woba bloo ba blah!" Their hair and their clothing flap and whip. Their skin ripples. Sarah laughs, but her giggles get blown away. Doctor Zhao gets tangled in his pockets. Mara, grim-faced, just tries to keep them from falling over.

As quick as it started the blow dryer stops and the steam engine shuts down with a hiss, chug, chug, chug...chhhhhh... Then the walls ahead of them slide open.

Doctor Zhao's hair is a big puffball. Sarah untangles hers from her nose. Kreak crouches and hops, facing off against one wall, then the other.

Sarah laughs, "I think we just survived the people washing machine."

Doctor Zhao tries to push his hair down, but it poofs back out. "A bit unnerving, but we're certainly clean now."

"I was not prepared for that," Sarah says.

When the wall ahead of them fully opens, they walk forward. The next room thankfully has a normal door on the far wall. And in this room, on either side, the walls have floor to ceiling mirrors which oppose each other.

The group stares into the infinite hallway created by the two mirrors. Kreak shifts from side to side and tries to reach into

162

the mirrors.

"We look pretty good." Sarah says. She loosens a knot in Mara's hair.

Mara tries to see the faces of her mirror-selves, the many versions of herself she's not sure she'll ever be able to trust. She fixes her clothes along with the others, and then Doctor Zhao gestures for her to open the door.

Chapter 14: Progress

Looking out through the final door of the people-washing machine, Mara and her friends see what look like totally normal people. They're just walking by, normal city people on their way to lunch, or back to work, or on an errand or something. The people are in a plaza surrounded by little businesses with apartments above them.

"Wait," Mara says. "Are we still in the house?"

There's a guy hawking newspapers who shouts over the general buzz of the cityfolk. A few carts rumble through full of delivery boxes. Cars snort and whine in the distance.

"Okay then...." Sarah says, a bit confused. She takes a few steps out the door, looks around, then turns back to her friends. "Hey!" She points up, "You guys are in the belly of a dinosaur."

Mara and Doctor Zhao walk out to join her and look up. Kreak though, he creeps out. And when he sees the dinosaur, he leaps in front of his friends and throws his arms up. "ROAAARR!" he yells.

The cityfolk nearby jump back in astonishment. Sarah laughs out loud. Even Mara, still pretty upset, can't keep herself from.giggling.

"Whao, Kreak!" Doctor Zhao pats his shoulders. "It's not real, it's made out of fiberglass." He walks past Kreak and knocks on the giant brontosaurus.

Kreak's arms slowly fall. "Fiber grass?"

Mara reads the sign hanging around the dino's neck, "Bronto Burgers."

"Where the heck are we?" Sarah asks.

"We're in undercanyon," Doctor Zhao responds. "It's a decent sized town actually."

"Are we still in The House of the Human?" Mara asks.

"Yes, look way up above us, you can see we're still inside the mountain."

Far above them is a cavernous and craggy ceiling. It offers ample sunlight through a pocking of large holes. The town still has a shaded feel though—the lamp posts are on.

Suddenly, a boy shouts across the plaza, "TEL'GRAM FER DOC ZHAO! TEL'GRAM FER DOC ZHAO!"

The boy has climbed up one of those lamp posts and is surveying the plaza. Doctor Zhao signals at him, so the kid hops down and heads over. They meet him halfway across the plaza.

"Tel'gram fer Doc Zhao? Sign fer it."

Doctor Zhao signs, and the kid hands over a little yellow paper. Then he runs off before Doctor Zhao can say thank you.

Sarah points at the telegram. "It's all lines and dots."

Kreak looks over her shoulder, "Oooo, oooo, ah, oooo, oooo..."

"I can read this," Mara says.

"And how do you know Morse code?" Doctor Zhao asks with surprise.

"Uh...Nathan, a friend of mine, we learned it so we could write notes to each other in class."

"Who's Nathan?" Sarah tickles Mara.

Mara giggles a little and pushes her away. "Stop."

Doctor Zhao laughs with them. Then he says, "I'd think a teacher would recognize it."

"Right. So we'd draw pictures with the message."

Doctor Zhao rolls his eyes. "All right smarty pants, what's it say?"

The lines and dots '--. --- / -... . .-.. .-.. / -.-. ---' read just like letters to Mara. "It says, 'GO BELL CO.'"

"Go Bell Co?" Sarah says.

"That's it?" Doctor Zhao asks.

"Ya," Mara nods.

"Okay then." Doctor Zhao looks around. "I wish that kid hadn't run off. This telegram has no sender listed, and I don't know where Bell Co. is. I haven't actually spent any time down here in Undercanyon."

"Who do you think sent it?" Mara asks.

"I have no clue." Doctor Zhao says. "Hopefully a friend."

The plaza they're in is a patchwork of old wood planks here, cobblestones there, rough pavement which grows into sleek streets, and rotting wooden walkways that traipse themselves into sparkling cement sidewalks. Rustic road-stops share walls with paper and pen accountants. Classic cafes counter nouvaux restaurants, and the flickering of Edison bulbs in antique furniture stores stream into the ever changing LED projections emanating from gadget shops.

Mara touches the tip of her nose. "This is like every time."

"Seems to be a melange of modern history at the very least. Isn't it interesting?" Doctor Zhao says.

Sarah takes a step towards the flow of people. "Excuse me, we need directions?" Although most of the people bustle past, busy city style, an older couple on a stroll comes over.

"Hi! Thank you," Sarah says. "Do you know where Bell Co. is?"

The man scratches the bridge of his nose. "I think she means that old telephone company."

The lady frowns and shakes her head. "Of course she means the old telephone company. It's called Bell Co, you don't think maybe she's looking for the Tallmart?"

"Oh come on Thelma."

"Would ya tell her where it is, for gosh sakes?"

"Ya know!...Okay..Okay. Bell Co is right down that little walkway there at the end on the right." He points. "It's in the oldest part of town."

"Thank you so much," Sarah says.

"Oh it's our pleasure." The woman nods. Then she pulls her man along, saying to him, "There must be a costume party at Bell

Co. Just a lovely caveman costume, don't you think so honey?"

Mara and Sarah look at Kreak. He says, "Costoooom?"

The group heads in the direction the older couple indicated, and at the end of the walkway, they arrive at Bell Co. It's a rickety storefront with an old wooden porch. The handwritten sign on the door reads, *Please use window,* with an arrow pointing to the walk-up window which is shuttered close.

They step up onto the porch and Doctor Zhao taps the little bell on the windowsill. Ding!

Inside, they hear a chair slide back. Some boots walk across the floor and then the shutters pop open.

"Hi there," an old cowboy waves through the window. "Are ya interested in phone service?"

"No..." Doctor Zhao tries to reply.

"Free voicemail. People can leave you messages that you can listen to later." The cowboy flaps his eyebrows up and down.

"No, thank you though. No, we're here for a different reason," Doctor Zhao says.

"Ahh, ohh, all right." The cowboy looks pretty disappointed.

"Yes, we..."

"I don't get many people coming by anymore," the cowboy interrupts, brushing away some dust. Then he gives a big sigh. "Well what can I do for you then?"

"Yes, thank you, we..."

"Wait a minute!" the cowboy jumps in. "Are you Doctor

Zoo? I'll bet your Doctor Zoo."

"Why yes. I am Doctor Zhao."

"Well you got a message." The cowboy slaps the sill. "Not voicemail. I just wrote it down on a scrap of paper here somewhere. Seems like they were going door to door looking for you."

He pats his pants pockets, then searches through his leather vest. "Oh ya." He reaches up to his hat and pulls a little wad of paper out of from behind the band. He uncrumples it and reads, "'Doctor Zhao and Mara. Call me. The Lady Banks.' And then it's got the number for you to call." He touches down the note to the sill with his pointer finger.

Then he leans in. "Are ya interested in signing up for phone service?" he asks.

"Oh," Doctor Zhao says, "I guess we have to…"

The cowboy bursts into laughter. "Nah, nah, I'm just kiddin', it's a local number, y'all can use my phone." He keeps laughing as he plunks an old rotary phone onto the windowsill. "Heck, I didn't wanna fill out all that paperwork anyways. Have at it, holler when you're finished. Oh, by the way, Graham's my name, middle name… I like it better than my first."

"Well, thank you very much, Graham," Doctor Zhao says. Then he turns to Mara and nods at the phone. "Do you want to try talking to her? You might have better luck than I did."

"Oh." Mara scrunches her face. Then she shrugs. "Okay."

After blowing out a deep breath, she dials the number.

Ring...Ring...Ring...hisssss.

Then...

A familiar unfriendly voice comes through the phone, "The keeeyyyy."

"Um...hello?" Mara says.

"Little Mara," The greedy Lady Banks says in response, then she shouts, "Status Report!"

"Hey!" Mara huffs. "Um, we're looking for the next part of the key."

"The keeyyy..." The Lady Banks hisses

"We're looking for it! I think we're close."

Then, after a moment of silence, "The keeeyyy."

"You let me talk to Auntie!"

"Where are my people?" The Lady Banks asks sharply.

Mara scrunches her face. "What? You want to know about your soldiers?"

"Yes! Tell meee."

Doctor Zhao nods to Mara.

"Um, okay," Mara says. "Well, we ran into Carl and Chawz, and we also saw the twins, Greg and Craig."

"Put Carl on!"

"No, ah, he stayed in this, um, kingdom place we passed through. He wanted to stay there."

"Great… Well what about the twins? Are you with them?"

"Um…" Mara gulps. "No, they stayed on this island place…"

The Lady Banks hisses at her, then she suddenly shouts, "THE KEY!"

"Stop yelling!" Mara shouts back. "Geez. We're still looking, I just told you that."

The Lady Banks' voice gets hard as steel. "You have it."

"No. Listen, we're.."

"I Want The Key! I Don't Believe You! Now…" The Lady Banks suddenly changes her tone, sounding even more angry than ever before, "Captured! I WANT YOU CAPTURED!!"

Then with a loud CLACK, she just hangs up.

Mara gulps. She holds the phone at her ear for another moment, then she sets it on the receiver. "She hung up on me."

"Oh my. Okay. Mara, no, you did just fine." Doctor Zhao says.

Mara holds her hands over her sketchbook. She looks down at her front pocket. Then she throws her arms down to her sides.

Sarah hugs her as Mara takes a big stuttering breath. "It's okay Mara," Sarah says. "We'll save Auntie."

Kreak sways back and forth. He pats Mara on the shoulder. After Sarah lets go of Mara, he gently pokes Sarah. Sarah nods at him, so Kreak turns to the windowsill, reaches out, and gently presses down the button on top of the bell until the hammer swings up, "Binggggggggggg."

Graham returns to the window.

"Well I sure hope you had a good conver… Oh! Errm, looks like maybe not." He taps up the brim of his hat. "Well, sorry bout that. Mmm, y'all done here?"

"Yes thank you," Doctor Zhao tells him.

"Ya? Okay then." Graham reaches out to retrieve the phone. "Well if you don't need anything else, I'm just gonna express my condolences and say 'have a nice day', close these shutters here and go back to my tinkering. So... My condolences, and have a nice day." Then he closes the shutters.

"Wait, Graham!" Mara catches him, "We need help, we're lost."

Graham opens the shutters back up. "You sure do look lost. Well how can I help ya?"

Then he slams the shutters closed again.

Just a second later though, he opens the shop door. "Ya know what, y'all come in and grab some lemonade, take some weight off the feet fer a few."

They see why Graham works through the window, his workshop is overflowing with stuff. Shelves, cupboards, trunks, tables, everything is completely strewn with supplies, tools and half completed projects. Copper wire coils around glass tubes and fuses. Boxes spill magnets which suck nearby metal into porcupine piles. Stacks of phones climb up to compete with the chairs and bike wheels that hang from the ceiling.

"Have a seat," Graham says. "Help yourself to some lemonade." He motions for them to sit around the big table in the center that fills most of the room. "So how can I help you folks?" He plops down and begins to fidget with the project in front of

172

him.

"What're you making?" Sarah walks up next to him.

His contraption has a series of tuning forks connected to an old circuit board.

"It's a translation device that compensates fer scalar temporal misalignment."

"What's that now?" Doctor Zhao scoots his chair closer.

"Y'all know how everything really small sounds squeaky? Like mice or hummingbirds or crickets? Ya? Well they're squeaky cause they're actually talking really quick and they hear really quick too, and so this little gizmo sorts all that time difference out between us so we can talk to them. Well, at least I want to talk to them."

"Does it work yet?" Mara asks.

"Oh, I'm not sure ya know, still tinkering out some details. Ah... But what can I help y'all with?" He sets his tools down.

"Okay, yes," Doctor Zhao says. "We're looking for… What's wrong Mara?"

Mara reaches up to her front pocket. "It's beating." She pulls the little heart out. "There's a pulse."

Graham gets up, resets his hat, then comes round the table to Mara. She hands the heart to him and says, "This is the first part of a key. We're looking for the rest of it, but we don't know where it is, so we're trying to find someone named Nabu."

Graham hefts the little heart. Then he taps it, smells it, looks at it really intensely. He presses it to his ear, then against his forehead. He makes vowel sounds, "AaaahH HOOOOOAAAA UUUUUIIIIIEEeee EEAAAA." Then he shakes his leg.

"Maybe..." Graham hands the heart back, and looks around the room. He scratches under his hat, then wanders over to a shelf and plucks through a box. After a second, he pushes it away, and opens a trunk. He shuffles stuff around. "Nope, not here." Back to a shelf, then the table top, then he climbs up on the table and lowers down a satchel from the ceiling. "Nope." Off the table to a cabinet, then he pats his pockets down, then back to the trunk.

"Ah HA!" He reaches in and grabs something. "Heh, I made this doohickey a long long time ago. I've always wondered what it's for." He places it on the table.

It's about the size of a ping pong ball. It has eight coils of copper wire which wrap around a circular magnet and then arc down in veins to form a small sphere.

"See I think that little heart might fit through the hole in the magnet. Try it out." Graham nudges Mara.

Mara picks up the copper sphere and drops the heart through the magnet.

"Wowww," Mara says. The heart doesn't fall all the way to the bottom—it stops in the middle, flips itself upright, and then floats there, suspended right in the center of the sphere.

"Wow's right young lass!" Graham hoots. "Now that's an electromagnet, course it's not getting any current right now, but it still has a magnetic field and, hoo boy, it's phased just right for whatever that little heart is made outta."

174

Mara looks at Doctor Zhao.

"That's got to be the next part of the key," Doctor Zhao says.

"We found it?" Sarah claps.

Doctor Zhao nods. "I do. That copper sphere will fit perfectly into the circular depression on the vault door. "

Graham flicks his brim. "Well gobs, that's just neat. You gotta take it with ya now, that little heart belongs in there. No charge, it's on the house." He holds his hands up, grins and winks.

"Thank you so much," Mara says. "I mean this is huge. It's a huge help."

He gives her the thumbs up.

Then Mara remembers to ask, "Oh hey, do you know someone named Nabu? Doctor Zhao, we still need to find him, right?"

Doctor Zhao nods, "Yes, we do. There's supposed to be a third part to the key, although I'm not sure what it would be. So yes, we do need to find Nabu still."

Looking back to Graham, Mara asks again, "Do you know where Nabu is?"

"Nabu…" Graham looks up at the ceiling for a moment. "Nahhh... nope. But I gotta tell you, I don't get out much anymore, part of the story ya know."

"Oh, that's okay," Mara says.

But Graham cuts back in, "Actually, ya know, you might check with Wireless Co., back up in the plaza. These new fangled companies are opening left and right, but that Wireless Co., they been stealing my customers for a while now. Normally, I wouldn't send anyone to them, but they might actually be able to help ya. Point ya in the right direction. I'm a little outa the loop so to speak." He shrugs.

"Graham, that's great, extremely helpful," Doctor Zhao says.

"Well I hope so. Now, I gotta warn ya, they're gonna give you the run around at Wireless Co—big bureaucracy, lotsa papers, signing and such, not a little mom and pop shop." He sighs. "But I guess that's neither here nor there."

He leads his guests to the door with a big smile, "Y'all come back visit me soon now."

Mara and her friends thank him again and say goodbye. Then they head back up to the plaza, where big billboards tell them exactly where to find Wireless Co.

The oversized modern company doesn't disappoint Graham's description. It's in a towering skyscraper with the company name huge and high among the clouds. The lobby is air-conditioned and cool with high vaulted ceilings and a white marble floor that delights Kreak, but makes Sarah feel uncomfortable.

They sign in with the guard, who sends them over to the general information desk. From there, they wait through a series of nauseating lines filling out useless, confusing forms. Then they finally make it to the personal customer department, not the business customer department. But while they wait for the client search database representative, they're bombarded with opportunities to win random stuff. The catch is that they have to sign up for the company's mailing lists, or complete some survey, or maybe they have to open a Wireless Co. credit account.

Kreak was excited to accept the offers at first, but now he's cowering under a mountainous stack of opportunities. Panicked, he quickly tosses them all behind the bench they're sitting on and then looks bashfully at Sarah with his shoulders scrunched.

"It's okay Kreak." She pats him on the forearm.

Finally, finally, they sit down in an office across from an extremely nice young woman wearing a very sharp suit.

"Now I've been told that you four are interested in starting a wireless family plan and I can definitely help you with that."

Mara begins to swallow her brain, but Doctor Zhao cuts to the point, "We're looking for Nabu."

"Oh!" The woman blinks. "That has nothing to do with starting a family plan. Okay… Nabu… Is that someone you talked to in the personal marketing department?"

Sarah groans. They've answered that same question four times already.

Doctor Zhao asks again, insistently, "Do you know where Nabu is?"

The woman frowns. "You're kidding right? Look I can't help you find this Nabu person, or whatever Nabu is. Here at Wireless Co., we provide wireless services of all kinds for homes and businesses."

But then her wireless phone rings. She raises an eyebrow at the incoming number. "Hold on for a second please?"

She answers, but she doesn't say anything, she just listens. Then she rolls to her computer and clicks her mouse a few times. A tiny smile flashes on her face, then she hands Doctor Zhao her phone. "It's for you."

"Hello," Doctor Zhao says. His face tightens a bit. "Okay. We'll be out in front... Yes. Okay. We'll be careful. See you soon."

He gives the woman her phone back and says, "Thank you for helping us." Then he quickly stands up.

The woman says, "Like we say here at Wireless Co., 'Doing business with Wireless Co. means you're great!'" Then she adds, "And I can assure you that I have absolutely no memory of the person you never mentioned to me just a few moments ago."

Doctor Zhao nods, then he leads his friends out of her office.

As quickly as he can, Doctor Zhao rushes them back through the hallways and down the elevators and escalators until they're once again breathing non-filtered fresh air in the plaza. Only then does he pause so they catch their breath.

"That was Nabu on the phone."

Chapter 15: Computations

Doctor Zhao looks out over the plaza. Wireless Co. soars sleek above them as a skyscraper should. They stand under its overhang, at the top of the few steps that lead down to the sidewalk.

"Well, what'd Nabu say?" Sarah asks.

"Naahhbuuu..." Kreak rolls the name around in his mouth like a piece of candy.

Doctor Zhao shakes his head, "He's sending someone to get us. I guess it's gotten bad. The Lady Banks has sent a small army into Undercanyon and they're looking for us. And Nabu said they've launched some sort of cyber attack also. We're supposed to wait here."

The normal flurry of the town's business district is bestranged. There's an unusual amount of people with hats on. People with hats linger in ones or twos or more. People with hats walk too slow for the sidewalks, or window shop the same window for too long.

Noticing this, Sarah says, "What's up with all these hat people?"

But just then, Mara suddenly cries out, "Hey!" And Kreak

spins around, startled. A bustle of hat people are right behind them. Hat people! And before Mara and her friends can do anything, hats are put on their heads.

The bustle of hat people start speaking at them, "Doctor Zhao." "Follow us." "Act normal." "They're coming." "Shhh!!" "Act normal." The bustle absorbs Mara and her friends into their stroll and sweeps them down onto the boardwalk. Doctor Zhao indicates with a flail to his friends that they should just go with it.

"What?" Mara lurches as she sees a weird looking Sarah staring back at her with huge eyes. Kreak bobs fiercely as they walk and he reaches for Sarah's face. Doctor Zhao says, "Oh my!" and stumbles for a moment. "Our faces look different!"

"It's the hats." The bustle of hat people respond. "Don't be alarmed." "The hats change your face." "Act normal." "It's the hats." The hat people continue to usher them down the sidewalk at a casual pace.

Mara and her friends all look different. Somehow the hats are changing the way their faces look, disguising them. Their noses and chins and lips, all their features seem to be shaped slightly different than normal.

Mara reaches up and feels her face. It doesn't feel like she's actually changed, but by the way her friends are looking at her, she knows she must look very different. "Wow," she says. Mara doesn't really like wearing hats, but this one's really comfortable even though she has no clue how it's making her face look.

They bustle along, and after a block or so, the hat people

chime up again, this time in a quick urgent flurry. "Act normal." "They're almost here." "Going for a stroll." "Boring office chat." "Now." "Now." "Act normal." "Here they come."

And then, in a hustle of footsteps and radio chat, the agents of The Lady Banks sweep around the corners from all directions at once.

The hat people strike up casual office conversations.

The collared-teed agents of The Lady Banks, with their jeans and belt devices, fan out and jog towards Wireless Co. They scan the crowds on the sidewalks as they pass.

Kreak hops and bobs.

"Calm down Kreak," Sarah whispers to him.

But Kreak is starting to freak out. He keeps hopping up and down, and he's staring straight at the collared-teed agents.

And they notice.

"Hey!" one of the agents shouts. "Is that the caveman?"

The nearest collared-teed agents head towards Kreak. But before they take five steps, all of the hat people start bouncing. Bouncing, bouncing, Mara starts bouncing too. Sarah, the hat people across the street too, they bounce. All of them, bouncy, bouncy, bounce, just like Kreak.

The agents skid to a stop. "What the heck is wrong with these people?" one of them says.

Just then, a black minivan squeals around the corner, then screeches to a halt. The side door slams open, and a woman leans out the door with a megaphone. "Get to Wireless Co. now! They're still in the building!"

"Look at the guy in the van," Sarah gasps.

Behind the woman, inside the van, a computer programmer with huge goggles and big fat gloves is hanging from the ceiling of the van, suspended by straps. He's making a continuum of obscure and mystic gestures, writhing and turning in the air.

Mara decides she's definitely gonna draw him! Oh wait... She remembers that she's not gonna be an artist anymore. Nevermind.

The van peels off and the agents in the road turn and sprint towards Wireless Co.

The bustle of hat people hustle Mara and her friends forward again. "Keep going." "Did you see their programmer?" "Almost there." "Don't worry." They chatter as they head down the sidewalk, a little faster now. "Common gear." "Doesn't compare with ours." "There might be more." "Act normal."

They pass office buildings and stables, a dental clinic, a blacksmith, and other businesses plucked from the time stream.

After a few more blocks, the hat people turn them into a 42 Hr Fitness Center. They breeze past the smiling receptionist and head down a side hallway where one of the hat people uses a key card on a door marked *Private Changing Room #3*. Then the whole group squeezes into the undersized changing room. "Made it." "Excuse me." "Close one." "Private Entrance."

One of the hat people struggles to get past Kreak.

Mara tugs on his arm. "Kreak, over here," she says. Kreak

shifts out of the way and the hat person squeezes past him and then punches at the number pad on a locker.

The locker door swings open. "Come on," the hat person says and ducks into the locker. One by one everyone squishes through the locker into a secret narrow hallway. At the end of the hallway, they climb a staircase that backtracks on itself several stories, until finally, they stand before a nondescript white door.

The hat people wait there without knocking. "One moment." "Someone will open it." "We're safe now." It's an uncomfortable minute though before the door bursts open.

A girl around Mara and Sarah's age, with long hair and a strange monocle shouts at them, "Quickly! Quickly! Inside! Activity Stations!" She turns and runs. The bustle of hat people run inside. Mara and her friends shuffle in. The door swings shut behind them.

They're in a massive room with a very tall ceiling. Above them, in the overhead space, a complex grid of spider fine wires tangles and weaves its way into every corner. Throughout the rest of the room, hat people of all ages, shapes and colors are deployed. They move wildly, gesturing with their hands and feet. Some stand, some sit in chairs, some lie on the floor, some perch on shelves and landings that crop out from columns or walls. Others hang, suspended in harnesses, moving their whole bodies in fabulous contortions.

"Holy moly," Sarah says.

"What are these people doing?" Mara asks.

The girl with the monocle sprints about halfway across the room before she notices that they aren't following her. So she leans hard to her left, executes a tight U-turn, and careens back towards Mara and her friends.

"Come on you guys, follow meee!!!" she yells. She leans hard to her left again, into another high speed U-turn and flies past them. Her hair slaps them in the face one after another.

Sarah shakes her head. "Geez. This is kinda crazy."

They chase the girl across the room to the origin of the complex wire array that fills the vaulted ceiling overhead. It's a pool of icy water, from which a thick column of twirled wires climbs upwards and then splays out into the spider fine grid. In the water of the icy pool float large clear balls that have circuit boards and microchips inside of them.

The girl with the monocle grabs a hat that's sitting on the edge of the pool and she slams it down on her head.

Doctor Zhao reaches up towards his hat, but the girl points at him. "Keep your hat on!"

Doctor Zhao bashfully lowers his arm back down.

Kreak touches Sarah's face. They all look like themselves again now, the hats are no longer altering their appearance.

"This is totally crazy," Mara says.

Even Doctor Zhao looks pretty shocked.

Mara and her friends can't see the man who is standing right in front of them. He has his camouflage activated. It's a computer program emanating from his hat that makes him blend in with his background. Standing very still, like he is right now, his camouflage makes him essentially invisible.

The man examines his visitors a moment longer, enjoying their looks of awe and confusion at his domain. Then he flicks his thumb in the air and shuts off his camo prog.

"AAH!" Mara yells when he suddenly appears right where she was looking. She stumbles back into Kreak whose eyes are popping out of his head. Sarah gasps too, while Doctor Zhao actually leaps back. "Ohhh!" he cries out.

The man standing before them is too tall to be called short, too thin to be called wide, bronze and brown and beige, strong and delicate; he's more like everything than nothing, but more like nothing than one thing. His hat fits perfectly.

"Travelers, I am Nabu. I am now going to awaken your hats so that we can work together. This will be unlike anything you've ever experienced. Prepare yourselves."

He taps a short rhythm on the sides of each of their hats. Mara and her friends instantly scallop and squirm as their surroundings digitize with a gleam. It's like the room they're in suddenly joined with a video game, or like they've traveled inside a computer program. Around them, the hat people, their movement makes a little more sense now as the digital objects and virtual control arrays that they're manipulating come into view. And above them all, the spider fine grid of wires is now filled with floating symbols and figures made of light, blocks of ethereal writing that twist and turn, and countless little creatures climbing and flying and crawling through the array.

"Oh my goodness," Doctor Zhao gasps.

"Holy moly!" Sarah says.

Mara and Kreak both look around in awe.

Nabu says to them, "With the help of my hats, you're now able to see the electromagnetic realm. Welcome to my headquarters."

Nabu's appearance has changed dramatically. No longer a simply dressed man in a hat, he's now covered with a complex outfit made of light. A flowing cloak covered in little objects and creatures is draped over his shoulders, and his hat emits a brilliant halo that floats above him.

"You look so awesome!" Sarah says. "What is up with your cape? What are those things? Are they alive"

Mara and Doctor Zhao still stagger as they try to assimilate this new digital dimension. Kreak is in a state of shock. He grabs onto Mara's arm for comfort, but she's too stunned to take his hand.

"Guys, isn't this amazing?" Sarah says. "Guys? Wow! Nabu, your cape is so cool!"

"My cloak of codes. These are my programs, and they are alive—in their own way," Nabu says.

His cloak of codes is magnificent and majestic. Programs crawl around his neck and flow over his shoulders, creatures of all shapes and kinds, crafted of light. They linger near his hands and sweep out behind him. Around the border of his cloak, earthy connectors writhe and coil. Filling the center, gentle blue processes sit eagerly waiting to input/output. But along with these more docile programs, fiery functions spark and flare. Windy widgets whip and bind.

Doctor Zhao is finally able to stammer out, "This is... What is... What is all of this?" He weaves a step and waves his hand around.

A smile flicks across Nabu's face. "Data. Information. Action. This is the electromagnetic realm."

"What's everyone doing here? What's happening out there?" Mara asks. The walls and ceiling seem transparent now and in the city around them, giant forms flow through the sky and explosions of color burst and flare.

"We fight against The Lady Banks." Nabu says. "She's launched a massive cyber attack, but we're doing everything we can to counter and thwart her. She's strong, but we are stronger."

Nabu's hats are truly powerful tools. More powerful than Mara and her friends can imagine. Every aspect of the physical world has been overlaid with the digital world of light. Mara watches the data streams in awe. It's the most glorious, scariest thing she's ever seen. In the city beyond the walls of the warehouse, lashing bolts of red root kits sear the sky and explode like depth charges. Gigantic shadow worms slither through buildings and dive into buildings. And high above, way up in the sky, massive swarms of queries bloat and snap.

Nabu's army of hat people sustain an impenetrable shield

of subterfuge and diversion. They bait The Lady Banks' malicious worms with phony servers. They distract the swarms of queries with fleeting false identities, and they launch hyper-accurate code clusters at the searing rootkits, desequencing their IP targets, causing them to flounder and fail.

"Horrific and beautiful," Nabu says, which is exactly what Mara's thinking. Nabu tilts his head. "In the cyber realm, we can hold them back forever. Their codes are weak compared to ours. But it isn't the cyber realm that I'm worried about. Those agents searching for you out on the streets of Undercanyon. They'll find my headquarters eventually. Which means that we're on the clock here."

But Nabu sees that his audience is having a hard time paying attention to him. He waves over the girl with the monocle, who comes and stands next to him. The girl looks totally different with her digital augmentations now visible. On her hat, a stack of programs gather. The programs tentacle out into telescopes and satellite dishes. Several codes segment her monocle towards Mara and her friends, examining them fiercely. A lot of the girl's programs sport lenses and microphones and antennae.

"HOLY MOLY!" Sarah yells out.

"This is so amazing," Mara says. "You look so… What are those things on your hat?"

Kreak roars, "AAAHRHRROOOEEAAIRG!!"

Doctor Zhao is trying to take some deep breaths.

The girl throws up her hands. "Pull it together people!

We've got work to do! On the clock! On the clock!"

But it's totally overwhelming, like being in a whole new world. Around them, Nabu's hat people are battling fiercely against The Lady Banks. They're stationed around the room working with bristling programming constructs. Bit by byte, the hat people feed massive functions into these constructs made of light. Library blocks hover close at hand filled with programs ready to deploy.

At core points in the room, cloaked groups of powerful looking hat people weave raw binary streams of ones and zeros into mystic machine language. On the tables and platforms these deadly figures surround, brand new functions are being compiled. As these new codes are completed, they slide or crawl or float around the room and hop into the defender's libraries.

The girl with the monocle hollers again, "Snap too! We've got work to do!" After she resorts to actually shaking and slapping Mara and her friends, they're able to settle down enough to hear Nabu.

He says, pointing to the girl with the monocle, "This is Mikayla. She's particularly good at finding things. She was the one who located the second part of the key."

Doctor Zhao raises his hand. "Wait, are you the one that sent us the telegram?"

"Yes," Nabu says. "As soon as I became aware of your adventure, I got Mikayla to start searching in the digital realm for the components of the key. Really, she wasn't having much luck until you guys found the first part, the little heart. We were able to see it when we tapped into your conversation with The Lady Banks in the cavern. This allowed Mikayla to focus her search." He pats Mikayla on the pack. "Pretty quickly she found the second part at Graham's shop. But unfortunately, we haven't been able to find the third part of the key. But with your help, we might be able to locate it together. Especially with your help Mara."

She gives him a confused look, but he just winks at her.

"But we don't have much time. We're on the clock!" he says. Then he whips around and heads towards a back corner of the room. "Follow me! Quickly now." From his cloak, a gang of friendly soft-toed programs hop down to the floor and spread out around Mara and her friends. With clicking murmurs and tumbling cartwheels, the little progs herd the group after Nabu.

He leads them to the corner, where a round glass table is covered with a few seemingly random objects. On one side of the table, a large globular fish bowl holds an excitable school of tiny fish that flit around a little ceramic castle surrounded by underwater plants. On the other side of the table is a heavy looking rectangle of solid grey metal. And in the center of the table, a necklace of black beads encircles an empty saucer.

But what's perhaps even more curious, is how normal the table looks compared to the rest of the room. While the rest of the room is a frenzy of electromagnetic activity, here in the corner, there are no data streams at all, not a single code at play.

Nabu taps the table, then he points at the empty saucer in

the middle of the table. "Mara, would you please place the key on the saucer?"

Mara nods and pulls out the little copper sphere with the heart in it. "Oh wow!" she says as she sees with her new perception that the little heart pulses with a soft pink light.

Nabu looks with awe at the key. "Truly beautiful. The work of a great artist."

Mara thinks it's beautiful too. But Nabu's words cause a little frown to flick across her face.

Before Mara can sink into that frown though, Doctor Zhao speaks up. "What is all this?" he asks, pointing at the table with it's odd array of objects.

A look of fatherly pride flashes across Nabu's face. "This is a quantum computer that Mikayla and I built. The special thing about this quantum computer though, is that it can read our minds, our intentions."

"Wow! Really?" Sarah asks.

"It sure can," Mikayla says. "But our intentions need to be really clear, really focused, or else it does weird things."

"Yes, we need to be careful not to waste our time with distractions," Nabu adds.

"This won't break the key?" Mara asks.

"Oh no, most assuredly not."

Mara nods and gently places the key on the dish.

"Now, everyone stand back." Nabu says.

They all take a step back as Nabu surveys the organization

of the table. He closes his eyes and stands very still. "This feels right," he says. Then he slows his breathing, and all the programs of his cloak settle and poise.

Nabu begins to make sound. First he emits a low thrum, and Mara and her friends watch in awe as a delicate field of code emanates from his gut. The gentle blue light of the code forms a feathery cloud around him, around them all. It fills the corner.

Then Nabu adds vowels to his chant. Roped binary streams of gold sweep out from his heart. The brilliant bands circle behind him and join together in the center of his cape where they encompass a single program into their grasp.

Nabu adds the clicks of consonants to the vowels and the bands gently lift their precious cargo up and over his head. The intensity of the bands delicate movement lights up the corner in sparks of bronze and vermilion. The bands of golden streams reach forward over the table and gently place the program down onto the key, onto the top of the tiny copper sphere.

Nabu stops chanting and the golden streams dissipate. He lets the thrum cease and the blue aura surrounding them dissolves.

On top of the copper sphere now, a beautiful program of pure green light sits very still. It looks like a very small human with a big belly sitting in the lotus position.

"Okay," Nabu says quietly. "This little prog that I've placed on the key is my philosopher's stone. An ever unfolding flower, it's the path of the traveler." Nabu still shimmers with traces of the powerful programs he just deployed. He relaxes his shoulders and seems to rest for several moments.

Then he whips around to face them. "Right! On the clock. So, as I said, this is a quantum computer, not a binary one– basically that means that this computer peruses possibilities as opposed to delineating data. So now, what we need to do is we need to intensely think about what we want, and we need to direct our intention towards those fish."

"The fish?" Sarah asks.

"They're exceptionally sensitive," Nabu says. Then to Mara, "Now Mara, the rest of us are going to focus our thoughts, focus our intention, but you, you're an artist, which means you're exceptionally talented at creatively expressing yourself. So while the rest of us think about our need to complete the key, I want you to…"

But she interrupts him, "Um, Nabu, I'm not really that good at… I'm not an artist anymore."

He looks confused. "Yes you are Mara. I've seen your drawings."

Mara shakes her head. "I'm not drawing anymore. I've given that up."

Doctor Zhao shifts uncomfortably.

Sarah puts her hand on Mara's shoulder, "Mara, you really are an excellent artist."

Mara shrugs Sarah's hand off and shakes her head. "No, I'm not." She frowns. "It's okay. I'm...uh...maybe I'm gonna be a doctor or something."

Nabu steps in front of her. "Mara. It doesn't matter what you say. You're an artist. You have the mind, the eye and the heart of an artist. This isn't something that you have a choice about."

Mara shakes her head at him, her face scrunching up, her eyes cloud up and she says sharply, "No! I'm no good. My drawings are scribbles. You can't make me draw. I'll hurt someone!"

"Oh Mara…" Sarah says.

Mikayla steps in front of Nabu and says, "Mara, it's okay! It's okay. You don't have to draw anything if you don't want to." Then she whispers something in Nabu's ear. He listens to her, then nods.

"Okay then," he says a little awkwardly. "I'm sorry, I didn't know. I was hoping you could use your creativity to help us think outside the box, but that's okay, you can just do what the rest of us do."

Mara doesn't respond. Her face is still all scrunched up and frowning, but she gives a little nod.

So Nabu goes ahead and arranges the group into a semicircle around the table. "Ok everyone, we've got to focus. The Lady Banks could find us at any moment. Focus is the name of the game here. I'm going to start the philosopher's stone program and once it gets going, allow me to guide your thoughts. We'll speak to the fish with our minds."

He stands in the center of them. His cloak finds its way as he moves, but now it spreads around behind them. "I need all of

194

you to clear your heads," he says, and then he flips his hands. His fingers come together, then pop apart, and from the two edges of his cape a splash of little link progs spill to the ground.

The tiny programs skitter into lines, forming snake-like cooperations that coil and inchworm their way up to the table top.

With flickers of data transfer, the links form a web on the glass table that joins together the fish bowl, the block, the necklace, and the copper sphere with the little heart.

On top of the key, in the center of the table, the philosopher program with the big belly rouses from its meditation. It yawns and stretches its arms, and looks around.

"Awesome," Nabu whispers under his breath. His eyes gleam with excitement as his creation comes to life. "Okay everyone, think about the key. Think about finding the rest of the key. Think about our need. Let all other thoughts drift away, let our need fill our consciousness."

Mara tries to let go of all her emotions—not easy—and just focus on the key, on her need to complete the key.

Nothing happens at first. The tiny philosopher is still doing warm up exercises.

"Keep clear folks. Keep as calm and quiet in your minds as you possibly can. Allow our need to complete the key to become our sole focus, our one and only thought." Nabu says.

The philosopher program finishes some waist circles and then it sits down and reassumes the lotus position, legs crossed onto each other. One hand settles onto its belly.

Then, a surge of frolicking electrons light up the web of links. Glowing fields and streams of data swirl around the philosopher's stone.

The sacred program raises its other tiny hand and with a great circle points one finger upwards. The roots of projection flourish in the heart of each black bead of the necklace that surrounds the dish. Light sparks and models above the philosopher. Small snaps and gleams form, but no true image coalesces. Substance is elusive.

"Think of the key. Think of our need," Nabu whispers. At his words the group focuses their minds even more. Sarah sees the key in her mind and she keeps repeating the world 'Complete! Complete!" Doctor Zhao visualizes the key turning in the depression on the vault door, he sees the vault door opening, opening, opening. Mara does her best to imagine the key, but she keeps seeing butterflies in her mind for some reason. As hard as she tries to clear her head, the beautiful winged insects keep fluttering past. Kreak, though, he is focusing on his needs quite clearly.

The sparks splinter and multiply, lines and fields begin to form above the philosopher. A scene takes shape!

It's a rough and scattered image. There are white bars above and below. The light draws and contracts into a bowl... It's a wooden bowl. The bowl is filled with veggies. Cut veggies and dip. Ranch dip!

Kreak bellows, "AarrgGGHH!"

"Mikayla!!" Nabu yells. "Take Kreak to the fridge and feed him please." The image above the philosopher fragments, then dissipates as Nabu pulls Kreak out of the circle. "Thank you Kreak, you did so well."

Mikayla leads Kreak away.

Nabu spins back around. "I guess Kreak's need was the clearest."

They regroup around the table. Nabu directs their attention back to the philosopher's stone, which sits patiently on top of the key. "Let's try this again. Focus on the key. See it complete. See the key."

They clear their minds and listen to the horizon of silence. They hold their need for the key as a quiet unobserved presence in the center of their cosmos.

Above the philosopher, the sparks once again heighten their vibration, the light evolves into lines and fields.

But nothing forms.

More nothing.

"Let's try thinking about the location of the final piece of the key now. We need to know where it is." Nabu chants into the rhythm of the light. "Relax deeper. Lose yourselves in your intention."

But nothing happens. There are sparks and waves of color, but they don't finalize into line or shape. It's almost like they are being blocked by something.

Nabu's momentary frustration ripples past until only his

calm remains once again. He gives himself a bit more space and begins a chant that flows his gut in blue light. Programs dance for position on his cape. A wave of seekers and snufflers leap to the table, their lenses and tentacular noses explore and sniff.

The lights above the philosopher's stone program orbit and alter contrast, but still no image.

Nabu adds chicks and chatters to his chant that sound like quaking leaves in the wind From his cape rise winged widgets with huge compound eyes, their ommatidia focus on the fractal reality.

Still nothing!

Nabu's frustration rips through his calm. "Focus!" he yells, "We're close!" Then he roars a deep bass sound and three powerful connector programs use their muscular arms to launch off his cape. The beasts flip through the air, their tails whip up to catch the rafters above, and they swing back and forth, pushing and pulling at the light.

Nabu's brute force attacks fail. His frustration roils around the table and shakes everyone's foundation. Their search leans over the precipice of doom. Mara begins to feel the fear of failure crawl up her back.

Then suddenly, an alarm blares in the warehouse, a commanding klaxon. "WoooOOOEEEEEEEeeeee! IMMEDIATE DATA SEQUESTRATION! WoooOOOEEEEEeee!"

"Nooo!" Nabu cries out. "We were so close!" He spins towards the big room. "Okay!" he says to the group. "They must have tracked us in the physical world. They're about to bust down the doors. We have four minutes to get the heck out of here. Mara, I'm going to recall the philosopher and then you grab your key."

"Wait!" Mara says. "We can't give up!" She rips at the snap of her pocket and pulls her sketchbook out. "I'll draw, I'll draw. I have an idea."

"Okay," Nabu says. "One more shot. It's all we have. Everyone go! 45 seconds! Mara draw your heart out!"

Quickly they focus back on the fish. In their desperation, their need is loud and clear.

Mara puts her purple pencil to a clean page and begins with huge arcs, vivid purple lines that cross the page. More lines and a form takes shape, a body and two huge beautiful wings. Antennae and legs. Beautiful and bold, the butterfly fills her page.

Auntie loves butterflies. Auntie loves to tell about how caterpillars grow into butterflies. With love and amazement in her voice, she tells of how the caterpillar takes and takes from the plant it grows upon. A parasite, it takes and takes and takes. But then the caterpillar gets to a point where it's taken enough. And then it builds a cocoon. And within that swirled enclosure of silk, the caterpillar completely liquifies itself, and then a miracle happens. From that strange jelly, a butterfly forms. It's a whole new creature. A beautiful creature with gorgeous wings. The butterfly climbs out of its cocoon and steps back into the light, and now, instead of taking and taking, it gives and gives. It helps the plant to spread its pollen so that new flowers can be born. The caterpillar transformed from something greedy and self-serving, into a beautiful and generous butterfly. Mara loves butterflies so much. She can feel her love flow onto the page. She can feel the joy she feels when she listens to Auntie's stories. And as Mara finishes the last lines of her drawing, she gasps as she feels tingles flowing through her. Purple sparks dance across her drawing!

With a twinge of fear, Mara drops her pencil and gasps. The lines of her artwork sear into sharp streaks of purple light. Her butterfly lifts off the page in a swirl of magic and color. It flutters amidst the purple glow and the sparkle surrounding Mara, and then it flies straight into the light above the philosopher's stone.

Panic rushes through Mara. She didn't mean to make the magic. Her breath catches as she imagines Nabu's computer exploding. She imagines her friends getting hurt. She imagines failing Auntie and Auntie getting blown up by The Lady Banks. In that frozen moment, all of Mara's terror consumes her.

Her butterfly splashes into the light above the philosopher's stone and bursts apart. The lines of its shape tear apart and sweep through the air in wild fantasy. Purple sparks dazzle and the lines sear the space above the philosopher. And then fields of multi-colored light coalesce. The lines of her drawing model into new forms and shapes, and three scenes appear in front of them.

"Mara, you did it!" Nabu shouts.

Pointing to the scene on the left, Doctor Zhao says, "That's globe island!"

"Where you found the first part of the key," Sarah adds.

Mara's panic is replaced by exhilaration. *It worked! It*

actually worked! She points to the middle scene, Graham sits at the table in Bell Co. tinkering away. "Graham!" she yells.

But as they all look to the third scene, a sense of shock runs through them all. The third scene is of a satellite floating in outer space.

"Outer space." Nabu says.

"Outer space!" Sarah exclaims.

Doctor Zhao points. "That's Auntie's satellite," he says. "It flies in geosynchronous orbit above the house."

"What's that mean?" Sarah asks.

"That means it stays directly above the house at all times." Doctor Zhao answers.

Kreak looks very confused.

Mara is shaking her head.

"But how are we gonna get there?" Sarah asks.

"I don't think we can," Doctor Zhao says.

"There's no way to win?" Mara asks.

But Nabu throws up a finger and says, "We have Spacebug!"

Then the klaxon blares again, even louder, "WOOOooeeeeEEEEEEEE!!! IMMINENT INVASION! BEGIN STERILIZATION PROCEDURES!!!"

The hat people had been working to preserve as many of their programs as possible, but now they back away from the libraries and the virtual control panels. Nabu's forces start moving now towards the back door. They scatter destro progs in their wake, vicious looking programs that skitter into the abandoned toolboxes and coding stations, where they wait for the signal to unleash their destructive force.

"Make it happen!" Nabu yells to his people. Then to Mara and her friends, "Quickly, let's get our stuff."

Mikayla skids up to them with Kreak in tow, who's loaded up with two handfuls of veggies.

Nabu blinks at Kreak, then he turns and focuses on the table. He begins to chant again, and his song carries his philosopher's stone back to the safety of his cloak. Then he recalls the rest of his programs—the beasts, the links—he chants all of them back to their places on his cloak of codes.

He shakes his shoulders to settle his cloak. "Quickly grab your key Mara, the bad guys are about to bust through the front door."

She grabs the little copper sphere and slides it into her front pocket with her sketchbook and snaps the snap tight.

Nabu rushes them towards the rear exit. As they move, he flicks out small, terrifying programs that hiss and creep to lurk and ambush.

The klaxon blares continuously now, "WOOOOOooeeEEEEEEEEE! EVACUATE! EVACUATE! IMMINENT INVASION!"

Nabu uses a program to amplify his voice, which booms through the room, as loud as the klaxon. "Everybody out now! Go Go GO!"

Mara and the Magic Sketchbook

In a normal volume again he says, "Mikayla, take our friends to Spacebug. Mikayla! Mara needs to be the pilot. The satellite is too small for Doctor Zhao. She can do it!" He claps his hands. "Go now! I'll be last to leave!"

"Boss," Mikayla stammers.

Nabu points at Mara. "You can do it, Mara." He winks at her.

Mara says, "Spacebug?"

Nabu doesn't answer though. He spins around and yells to the room, "Hold on to your hats!"

Mikayla's hands fly up and grab onto her hat. Mara and her friends copy her just as a huge boom rumbles through the room, shaking the building and causing them all to stumble. The front door explodes open and The Lady Bank's collared-teed agents burst in.

One of them yells through a megaphone, "Give us Doctor Zhao and Mara!"

As the agents pour into Nabu's headquarters, the last of the hat people dash to the back of the room. Nabu flicks a few dragonfly cutter progs up into the air. The swift little codes fly overhead into the spider-fine grid of wires and begin to chew and chomp and cut cut cut.

The agents of The Lady Banks slow down and look upwards as pops sizzle across the ceiling. The spider-fine grid shivers. Then with a wild whip and and snap, the whole complex array of wires collapses down to the floor. The lurking destro progs trigger, and with a ripple of explosions, they unleash their fury. Panels burst, sockets shock, consoles crack and crumble. The collared-teed agents retreat back from the chaos as the warehouse fills with smoke and tangle and sharp.

"Go Mikayla!" Nabu yells. His hands twist and turn, a horde of vicious progs rise from his cloak.

Doctor Zhao and Kreak watch in awe. But Mikayla pushes them towards the door. "Snap out of it!"

Sarah drags at Mara. "Come on sister!"

The group rushes out the back door into the quiet hallway of an office building. Mikayla hustles them onwards through the halls. They pass named and numbered doors. Hat people dash this way and that.

After a few turns, Mikayla screeches to a halt in the middle of the hallway. "Riiggghht here," she says. She reaches up and tap taps up high on a normal looking part of the wall. A hidden door clicks open revealing a secret elevator.

The elevator has only two buttons, one for this floor, that's marked with an *N*, and one for the basement, marked with a *B*. But Mikayla taps open an even more hidden panel, a tiny one near the floor on a side wall. Then she pushes the super secret button marked with an *S*.

"Um… Mikayla," Mara asks. "Spacebug?"

Chapter 16: Outer Space

As the elevator rises, Mikayla collects their hats and hangs them on hooks in the elevator. "We won't need these anymore."

They all blink and squint as they readjust to normal vision.

Then Doctor Zhao says, "I really don't think Auntie would want Mara to go in this spacebug."

But Mikayla shakes her head. "Doctor Zhao, you heard Nabu, you're too big to crawl into the satellite. It's got to be Mara."

Mara pipes up, "Doctor Zhao, you've got to let me do this. It's our only chance to save Auntie."

Doctor Zhao shakes his head. But after a moment, he lets out his breath and says, "I know we need the key, but..."

"I can get it," Mara says firmly.

"How safe is it?" Doctor Zhao asks Mikayla.

"Very safe," Mikayla nods. "Very safe."

Doctor Zhao throws up his hands. "Your aunt will definitely fire me."

"No she won't," Mara says.

Mikayla cuts in as the elevator slides to a stop, "Great! We've made up our minds then."

Doctor Zhao then surprises Mara when he turns to her and says, "I believe in you, Mara. You can do it."

She gives him a big hug.

The elevator has opened and now they all step out into the super secret top floor of Nabu's headquarters. It's a huge open room, much like the lower level they were at before, but it's fairly dark. Little lights lap at their feet. On the ceiling, lasers and pinlights project a realistic planetarium of twinkling, gleaming stars.

On one side of the room, Spacebug is cradled in a sling. She is a spaceship, a tiny graceful craft, and when the group enters, she purrs and blinks her lights at them.

"Hi Spacebug," Mikayla waves.

Spacebug looks a lot like a ladybug, except she's sleek and silver and gold. Mara thinks she's the cutest spaceship in the whole world. It makes her miss her aunt fiercely. "Come on guys," she says. "We have to save Auntie."

"Right," Mikayla says, then she yells towards the other side of the room, which is pretty dark. "Nikola!"

As soon as she calls out, a pint sized holographic human in a dapper suit with fairy wings poofs into the air right in front of them. Mara and her friends all gasp as he appears. Kreak even roars.

The little man looks a little insulted by their response, but once they recover, he gives them a huge bow and with a flourish of his hand says, "Nikola, at your service. Mikayla, I'm so.."

But Mikayla interrupts him, "No time Nikola. It's an

emergency. I need you to help these guys get Mara suited up and trained, and also help me prep Spacebug for flight."

"You want me to split in two?" Nikola harps. "I'm an artificial intelligence, not a magical creature, I'd like to remind you."

Mikayla throws up a menacing finger at him.

"Fine!" Nikola says. Then he writhes and blurs and finally pops in two.

"New guy only gets one word though," the original Nikola says with a grin.

"That is not ok," Mikayla counters.

"That it is!" original Nikola intones.

"What?" Mikayla gasps. "No. Geez!" She huffs, points at original Nikola, and says, "You come with me!" Then she storms over to several consoles across from Spacebug.

New Nikola looks at Mara and her friends. New Nikola squirms and frowns, and then points to the far side of the room and declares: "That."

He leads them over to a changing area where spacesuits hang in the corner. Along with the suits, a stack of giant flashcards leans against the wall.

New Nikola points Mara towards the smallest suit. "That." He squirms, then he points towards the flashcards. "That."

The next few minutes are a scramble of frustrated, "That"s, and head shaking and squirms from New Nikola. Following the instructions and diagrams on the flashcards, they all help Mara buckle and zipper her space suit on.

Back across the room at the consoles, Mikayla wakes up Spacebug and runs the pre-flight tests on her systems. "Bring up Auntie's satellite!" she finally orders.

The planetarium effect on the ceiling shifts and zooms, and for a moment, everyone glances up.

The image of a little satellite with lazy solar panels moves to the center of the ceiling.

Mikayla calls across the room to Mara, "Spacebug will take you up and dock with the satellite Mara. She knows where to go. All you have to do is crawl inside the satellite and grab the third part of the key. Hopefully it'll be obvious to you, whatever it is. Then you get back in Spacebug and she'll bring you home. Easy Cheezy."

"Okay," Mara says.

More buckling and zipping, New Nikola is like a miniature floating disco dancer that can only say one word. "That!" Point. "That!" Point. "That!"

Mikayla yells again, "Hurry up! The bad guys are close! We launch in two minutes!"

"Bad guys?" Sarah asks.

New Nikola spasms and flies so fast towards the flashcards that he splashes right into them with a sparkle. He pops back out and points at the cards. Sarah flips through them, but he keeps shaking his head until, "That! That! That !" New Nikola hollers and points with both hands.

208

Mara gulps.

"That!" Nikola double points.

It's the card with instructions for the ejection lever.

Moments later, they click Mara's helmet on. The group rushes over to Spacebug and they help Mara climb into the cockpit, and they strap her into her seat.

"You can do this Mara," Sarah says and then slams the hatch closed. She gives Mara a big thumbs up.

Mara nods. *I can do this,* she thinks to herself. But her heart is beating so fast. *I'm in a spaceship!*

Mikayla calls for Doctor Zhao, Kreak and Sarah to join her back at the consoles, then she flips on the intercom. "Check. Check. Mara, can you hear me good?"

"Ya," Mara says.

"Your mic works great. Ready?"

"I'm ready." Mara settles into her seat. Her sketchbook jabs her, but she's glad she has it.

Spacebug purrs.

The ceiling petals open and daylight floods in.

"Hold on Mara!" Mikayla calls. "Okay, go for it Bug!"

Loud clicks sound and two poles shoot up and stretch tight the huge rubber sling that cradles the craft.

"Wait, really?" Mara gasps.

Ka chik! Bwangwangwangwang!

The giant slingshot flings Spacebug and Mara through the roof with a wild rush of power. Mara's face smears towards her ears. She's never felt such an intense rush of speed. If she could scream she would, but her breath is totally caught.

Spacebug shoots up from Nabu's headquarters, right through an opening in the cavernous roof of Under Canyon. Through the window of the cockpit the sky blurs and streaks as the ship screams towards the stars. Into the sky, higher and higher up from the House of the Human, farther and farther above the coastal range. Spacebug splashes through the clouds, and then with a whirr and a click, she spreads her gossamer wings. With a roar, she flares her engine and begins to climb on a pillar of fire.

Mara says, "She's started shaking really bad."

"That's rocket power Mara," Mikayla says. "Hold tight, it's gonna last a few minutes."

Mikayla clicks off the intercom. "Phooey," she says. "Nikola, close the roof quick."

The giant slingshot retracts and the hatch in the ceiling closes.

"Look at this screen guys." Mikayla brings up video of the building's roof right above their heads. On it they see that The Lady Bank's collared-teed agents have used grappling hooks to climb up the sides of the building and are swarming over the edge onto the roof.

"What are they trying to do?" Doctor Zhao asks. "Can they get in here?"

Mikayla shakes her head. "No, I think we're safe in here. This room's pretty hard to find, and even harder to get into."

She clicks the intercom back on. "Mara, how's it going?"

"Fii .. ii. .i..i..inn..nee... Sh..shhh..haa..aak..king."

On the building's roof, the agents of The Lady Banks gather to one side. Then a huge container flies up from the street and lands on the roof. BAKOOM!

"Holy moly!" Sarah cries out. "That shook the whole building!"

"Wh.a..a.ts s haa.ap.pp enn. ing?" Mara asks.

"The bad guys are on the roof here. Just hang in there girl," Sarah says.

The collared-teed agents pop the top off the container, and the sides fall away. A very fat missile stands there.

"Oh my goodness," Doctor Zhao says. "Mikayla, what can we do?"

Kreak bellows, "Aaaarrggh!"

"Mara! They've got a missile!" Sarah shouts.

Mikayla starts punching at the consoles. "Spacebug! Get ready to defend yourself!"

Inside the little spacecraft, Mara feels like she's in a blender getting ripped apart. It's shaking so much, she can barely hear her friends. They have far off voices that may or may not matter. Mara's riding the wild between Earth and Space. Pounding fierce, bottom of the waterfall, top of the world. She grips her straps. Her surroundings, her reality, the readouts on the ship's screens, the lonely satellite, Auntie, the key, her sketchbook, all whorl away into the lost galaxies of scattered consciousness.

"Mara! Can you hear us?" Doctor Zhao asks.

Mara groans. Her teeth chatter. She tries to… Panicked future… She tries to focus... She.... Now she's... Time is… Space is… Now! Focus! Towers and domes, sparkles in the hillsides! Auntie! Auntie!

Mara cries out, "I.ii.ii wi..will s.s..ave you!"

Down below her on the roof of the building, The agents of The Lady Banks climb back over the edge of the roof, and the missile roars to life.

"Mara!" Sarah screams.

The missile launches. It tears upwards through the cavern ceiling of Under Canyon. It sears through the sky, ripping through clouds.

Red lights flash inside Spacebug. Alarms blare.

"Spacebug's gonna dodge!" Mikayla yells.

"Hold on Mara!" Doctor Zhao shouts.

Spacebug's instrument panel lights up with alarm. Her engine roars and Mara gets pressed even further into her seat. The atmosphere rips and tumbles against Spacebug's sides as she sprints towards space.

Mara asks, "Wh. uh. hu t ot. un iiiii eee iii…" But then she just tries to hold on.

"Missile incoming Mara!" Mikayla screams.

Spacebug suddenly swerves hard. Mara crashes to the side. The sceens blare information at her, but the words smear like comets.

212

But the missile follows Spacebug's turn. It gains on them. Bug spews out a huge cloud of sparkling foil.

The missile veers past her distraction. It closes in.

Spacebug soars and kites. She dives and blusters. Finally she throws everything into a last desperate crush for outer space. She flies faster than she's ever flown before.

But the missile's faster.

Bug readies for impact. Her systems shudder. Mara holds her breath.

Suddenly the missile explodes into five rocket warriors. They're viciously armored. Dark soldiers of the sky. The warriors flare their jetpacks. Flames spread like wings behind them. They boost towards Spacebug.

The dark soldiers latch onto the little ship and begin tearring at her. Bug shrieks as they rip at her shielding. She whips and bucks.

Mara presses her eyes shut. She grips her straps even tighter. What else can she do? With her fists, she can feel her sketchbook through the spacesuit, snapped tight in her front pocket.

A tear rolls down her left cheek. The tear jilts and stutters with the shaking of the ship. In that one single tear though, like in all tears, is a song. And far, far away, deep in her grotto in The House of the Human, Seergart hears this song, the song of Mara's tear, whispering down to her from on high.

"Mara," Seergart says aloud. Then after a deep inhale, she

sings a long high D note.

The tone soars around her grotto and whips up through a hole in the cavern ceiling and pierces the sky. The air around Spacebug ripples with the sound of Seergarts song. Then the note dives into Mara's ear.

Mara's eyes flash open. Immediately, instinctively, she hums her sacred tone.

Strong.

Her mind clears and her eyes see the one word that Spacebug is spilling across her screens. She hears the one word her friends are shouting.

"Eject!" Spacebug screams.

"Eject!" Mikayla yells.

"Eject!" Doctor Zhao and Sarah shout.

"Ejeck!" Kreak roars.

The rocket warriors glare at her and bang on the big window of the cockpit.

Mara yells at them, "Stop it! Let me get the key!"

But they can't even hear her. Mara sees that they're mindless warriors following stupid orders. She shudders. They're so scary looking with their faces barely visible through the dark black helmets.

Her breath quakes. She reaches up and touches her sketchbook through her spacesuit.

But even she could get her sketchbook out, and even if she wasn't shaking apart, what would she draw?

The dread warriors slice and bash at Spacebug. They tear and pry at her shielding.

What could I draw?! She's so scared, she can't think of anything. *An artist would be able to think of something.*

The warriors yell at her, but she can't hear them. They bang at the hatch.

Mara scrabbles at her spacesuit, but she's strapped in so tightly, there's no way to get to her sketchbook.

Dark clouds fill her head. There's no way forward.

Mara freezes, her breath freezes.

Sarah's voice breaks through, "Come on sister!" Sarah yells.

Mara looks up through the hatch and shakes her fists at the warriors. "Take this!" she yells. Then she reaches down, grabs the yellow ejection lever, and yanks it.

Little pops, snaps, and micro-explosions enter the orchestra of chaos. Then a hiss. A bang! And the hatch explodes outwards. Mara's seat ejects upwards, and she shoots high above the frenzy of her spaceship.

Below her, Spacebug begins to swerve and lose control. The five rocket warriors flare and jump off the ship towards Mara.

Spacebug, in one last momentous act, screeches and then in a fantastic explosion, she self-destructs.

BOOOOOM!

The shockwave from the explosion slams into the rocket warriors and jars the fire right out of their jetpacks. They float, stunned. Then they tumble down through the sky.

But the shockwave slams into Mara also. One of the straps holding her to the ejection seat rips loose!

She swings away from the seat, grasping the broken strap. Her feet sail up behind her. Her grip slides. She tries to get a hold with her other hand. She slips more. Then, yes! She grabs onto it tightly with both hands!

But just then, the seat's parachute deploys. The chute snakes up with a hiss.

"No..." Mara sees it coming, She holds on as tight as she can.

The canvas catches air, the ropes pull taught, and when the parachute pops open, it yanks the seat up with a sharp jerk.

The strap rips out of Mara's hands.

"NOOOO!" she screams.

Then she falls.

Tumbling. Falling. Clouds and stars and Earth. Clouds and stars and Earth. Mara chokes on her breath. Her head lolls and jars in her helmet.

She was going to be a great artist. She was going to inspire people.

Clouds and stars and Earth.

Her hands grab mindlessly. Her body twists with no idea where to turn.

Help me Auntie!

My sketchbook, my sketchbook...

Mara shifts. Suddenly she's able to catch her fall. Like a skydiver, she shoots her arms and legs out and begins sailing down on her stomach. The wind rips at her spacesuit, but her mind is able to settle just a little.

She can see the warriors falling through the sky beneath her. They're far away. They look like tiny flailing spiders.

Mara grinds her teeth and growls. She's got to draw something.

Maybe parachutes. But what if they don't work? What if they fall apart, or the knots aren't tied right? How do I draw the knots?

"Come on, think of something," she whispers.

An umbrella? A parachute. Come on! Wings! Yes! No. Would that even work?

The ground is getting closer and closer.

"I can't think of anything!" She flaps her hands, but it doesn't slow her down. Her heart is pounding so hard she can feel her sketchbook with each beat.

Auntie!

The warriors are panicking, legs kicking, arms flapping.

They're all gonna go splat.

Because Mara isn't creative enough. She's Miss Scribbles! Miss Scribbles! Mara's tearing herself apart inside. *An artist would be creative enough... AN ARTIST WOULD BE CREATIVE ENOUGH! AN ARTIST WOULD...!*

But then suddenly, Mara relaxes.

"Maybe..." the word whispers from her lips.

Quickly, she unclips her helmet and shakes it free. She clicks loose her gloves—they spin into the air. She unbolts the seam at her waist—the top and the bottom of her space suit slide off and flutter away.

The wind frenzies her hair. Her overalls slap her socks. Mara curls herself into a tight ball and unsnaps her front pocket. She carefully slides her sketchbook out. It flies open, pages rip and blow away. Mara wedges her sketchbook into the crook of her left arm and she sweeps a clean page into her grip. She pulls her purple pencil out of her pocket.

Glancing below her, the ground is rushing closer. The warriors tumble and flail.

"I need to save them too," Mara says.

Racing towards the ground, wind rushing, heart beating, sun shining, Mara sketches in her sketchbook.

Chapter 17: Heart

Falling, wind fierce and racing towards the ground, Mara draws. Onto the page of her sketchbook, with her favorite purple pencil, she draws beautiful bold lines with corners that connect clean. She shades and she shadows so the light can shine bright. She models her forms, and her drawing gains depth and substance. The wind screams, but to her, it's quiet.

Each line is filled with meaning. Her passion, her love, her need flows onto the page. And with her final stroke, she lifts her pencil, and looks at her drawing.

Windy real tears creep at the edges of her eyes.

Mara might've been a real good doctor.

She looks past the edge of her book at the approaching ground. Buildings are like bugs now, and the shapes of the land are making a lot more sense.

She looks back at her drawing.

It's like the feeling of a clear breath. It's like blowing sand from her hand, sinking her toes into warm mud, touching a jello cake. It's that moment where you float at the top of a swing, the splash when you jump into water, the warmth on your face when you look up at the sun.

Her sketchbook shimmers, a million versions of purple, and then it flares bright. A brilliant flash fills the sky, and she shines. For these few moments, Mara is the shooting star. The purple light that people will remember for centuries. The star of change.

Sparks dance around her. Like fireflies and fairies, they fill the air, swirling, shining, gleaming.

On the page, bolts of purple race through her strokes. Her contrast sharpens, her shapes swell and rise from her sketchbook.

"Yes!" Mara whispers. She brushes the hair from her face and her pencil slips from her hand. She grabs for it, but it flips away. Pages slide from under her grip and tear off into the sky.

Mara takes a deep breath, then she lets go of her sketchbook. It flutters next to her like a swamped gull, then it's gone.

The ground is approaching so fast.

Mara rolls onto her back. She throws her arms and legs out, and she falls.

And falls.

And falls.

And falls!

And... Sploooooooooshhhh!

She lands on the giant marshmallow!

The marshmallow sponges beneath her, pops her back into the air a little and then catches her again with a wobble.

"Wow," Mara says. She lays there for a few minutes bouncing gently up and down as the marshmallow settles.

High up in the sky above her, something gleams. The lonely satellite? Mara pats her pocket. The snap's closed and the copper sphere with the little heart is still there. She wonders if it will be of any use at all.

She tries to jiggle her way up to her feet, but decides to plop back down onto her belly and squirm to the edge of the marshmallow. She's in Auntie's garden. Spread throughout the flowers, the five other marshmallows she drew quiver and shake as the rocket warriors climb off of them.

Mara purses her lips, then she throws her feet over the edge and slides down the side.

The warriors shed their armor and jet packs and return to their standard collared-teed outfits.

"There she is!" one of them shouts.

Mara walks to an open spot and waits.

The agents rush over and surround her.

"Are you okay?" the same guy asks her.

"I'm Mara," she says, glaring at him.

"Good. You're coming with us."

"I want to see my aunt."

"We're taking you to The Lady Banks."

Mara raises her eyebrow. "Fine. Let's go then."

"No tricks." The agent points at her.

She glares. "Just take me to the Lady Banks."

The agent shakes his head at her, then he leads the group off with Mara in the center.

They cross the garden and go through the front door with its stained glass window of Earth. They travel through twisting hallways. Up and down spiraling staircases. They ride elevators and snowmobiles, and after a series of slides and swings, they row canoes to a stilt town in a cedar swamp. From there, a gondola carries them above a village with a reindeer farm, all the way past a gathering of waterfalls to the town of Choose Again. Then it's just a short walk to the side door of a humble warehouse.

Over the door is a heading, 'Future Sprockets and Such, Inc.'

The agent opens the door to reveal a narrow set of earthen stairs that lead upwards.

"Go on up." He says.

"Auntie's up there?"

The agent nods. "They're all up there."

Mara bites her lip, then furrows her brow. She takes a deep breath and hums a D note a couple of times quickly. Then she passes through the door and heads up the stairs.

The stairwell is little more than shoulder width at first, but it soon widens. Mara notices that the stairway seems to evolve as she climbs up it. Earthen stairs give way to rough cut logs, then to wooden boards. The stairway curves up into chiseled stone, smoother and smoother. Mara's mind wanders back over her journey through the House of the Human. The stairs shift to metal, sounding more loudly beneath her feet. Just like the house, the stairs seem to be carrying her through time, from the time of dinosaurs, to the era of kingdoms, and on into the industrial age with its spinning wheels and steam engines. The stairwell gets wider and wider. And as if she's moved into the modern age of computers and spaceships, the steps become plexiglas with laser lights that dance underneath her footsteps. And then a flicker of a smile runs over Mara's face as she feels the gentle softness of green moss carpeting the final rise of stairs. It makes her wonder what the future has in store.

She steps off the stairs into a large circular room, and of all the people gathered in the room, the first person she sees, sitting directly across from the door, is Auntie.

Auntie stands up from her chair and raises her hands to her heart.

"Oh my dear girl. Oh Mara, Mara, I was so worried about you." She reaches out with her arms.

Mara runs towards her and jumps into her Auntie's embrace. "Auntie!"

"Mara, Mara, Mara." Auntie holds her tight.

Mara presses her face into the flowers of Auntie's dress. The wool of Auntie's shawl is so soft against her cheek. And for just a moment, there's no invaders, there's no key, there's not even her sketchbook. There's just that feeling Mara gets whenever she hugs her aunt—that everything is okay.

"Thank goodness Mara," Auntie says. "Let me look at you." She holds Mara's face in her hands. "What would your mother say if she knew what I've gotten you into."

Doctor Zhao, Kreak and Sarah, who'd been sitting near Auntie, crowd close.

But then Mara feels a cold grip on her shoulder that pulls her away from her friends. A look of fear spills across Auntie and her friend's faces. Kreak growls.

Mara gets spun around and she finds herself facing a mean looking woman with sharp, arrogant features. The woman is wearing dark, flowing, very expensive looking clothing, it can only be the greedy Lady Banks.

The Lady Banks lets go of Mara's shoulders, looks her up and down and says, "Enough pleasantries my dear."

The big circular room is colored in bronze creams with brown furniture. The carpets are warm, the sunlight spills through the windows of an overhead cupola. There's a small kitchen nook, and a few doors leading to what Mara assumes must be a bathroom and some closets. The chairs and couches look comfortable. But the most impressive feature in the room is the huge vault door which dominates the whole back wall.

The vault door is massive and Mara can tell it's very thick and powerful. It's made of some metal alloy which swirls with copper and steel. There are no knobs or handles, there's only a simple round impression, exactly the size of the little copper sphere in Mara's pocket, just like what Doctor Zhao described.

Along with the Lady Banks is that gaudy group of people that Mara identified as the leaders of the invaders. They examine her with hunger and impatience.

Mara doesn't know who they are, but they definitely look like bad people to her. They're the faces behind the curtains that you never want to meet. The world's worst corporate overlords. L. Martin profits off of war. Boheme Grove lives off of lies. The Brothers K. enslave with scarcity. And Ms. Pfiz, she thrives off of sickness.

Mara huffs at the Lady Banks, "Why'd you stop me? I was gonna get the last part of the key."

The Lady Banks gives her a heartless smile. "So glad that you're safe, Mara."

Mara blinks at her. "You can talk normally, I see."

"Yessss," the Lady Banks hisses. "The keeeyy…"

Mara wags her finger. "Don't you start…"

The Lady Banks holds her hand out. "Give me the key."

Mara looks up at Auntie, who nods.

Mara unsnaps her front pocket. "It's not complete. I was going to the satellite to get the last part when your stupid rocketmen…"

The Lady Banks flaps her hand. "We'll see about that."

Mara pulls out the copper sphere with the little floating heart.

The Lady Bank's cronies edge closer.

Mara looks up at her aunt. "Auntie, I didn't get to the satellite. What about the last part of the key?"

Auntie looks concerned. "I don't know Mara."

The Lady Banks grabs the key out of Mara's hands and

examines it. "It doesn't matter," she says. "If it doesn't work, we're gonna strap your aunt to the door and L. Martin is gonna blow it open."

Mara screams at her "NO! No you won't!" She lashes out at the Lady Banks, but L. Martin grabs her wrists and holds her tight.

"Oh yes I will," the Lady Banks says to her coldly.

Mara struggles for a second, "Let go of me!"

But L. Martin doesn't let go, and his grip is like steel.

She finally stops struggling, her breath heaving now, tears at the edge of her eyes.

The Lady Banks walks over to the vault door with the key. "Now let's see if this key works."

She looks back at the group of people behind her, scanning the watching eyes of her cronies, of Auntie and her friends, of Mara. Then she turns and places the little copper sphere into the circular depression on the door.

She steps back.

A moment passes.

But nothing happens.

Another moment passes.

Then the Lady Banks turns back around and with an angry look at Auntie says, "So much wasted time! L. Martin, prepare your explosives."

"No!" Mara shouts. "Wait! Please! Let me try... I... I think I..." In that moment, Mara remembers the words of the Oracle—

Spin the heart with your heart... "Let me try," she pleads.

The Lady Banks stares at her for a second, then reaches back and grabs the copper sphere. She walks back to Mara and hands it to her. "Surprise me, little girl."

Mara looks down at the key in her hands. She approaches the huge vault door.

She hears the Oracle's voice in her head, *"Spin the heart with your heart..."*

As she stands in front of the door, Mara hears another voice. A voice only she can hear. Its words rise from deep within the mountain range and whisper into her ears.

"Who are you, young artist?

What path will you walk?

What will be your fate?

Will you enslave?

Or will you liberate?"

Mara somehow knows these questions aren't to be answered, but to be asked.

She shivers at the poem's call. She cradles the copper sphere with the little heart in her palms. Then she takes a deep breath.

Her back tingles as everyone watches her.

She looks over her shoulder at her family. Auntie nods at her. So does Doctor Zhao. Sarah smiles encouragingly, she really does feel like a sister. Kreak bounces and hits his fist against his chest.

Mara smiles at them.

Please work! She thinks to herself.

She looks over her other shoulder at the greedy Lady Banks and her cronies.

Then she turns back to the vault. Her heart is pounding so hard. She holds the key up. The heart looks so real. It floats right in the center of the sphere of copper wire, haloed by the circular magnet above it.

In her mind, Mara sees Tepe, swaying back and forth on the top of the mast, pointing out across the ocean. Then she hears the Oracle again, *"Spin the heart with your heart..."*

In her mind, Mara sees her father and her mother. She sees Auntie and her friends, Sarah and Doctor Zhao, Kreak. She pictures The House of the Human.

And in Mara's heart, an image of Earth grows. It's vibrant with plants and animals, with people who hope and dream and love. She can feel their stories. Each individual life is a tiny universe.

In her hands, the key shivers. The heart slowly begins to turn. Around and back, it turns, picking up speed. It spins faster and faster and faster—until it finds its beat.

Mara's own heart matches the beating of the tiny heart. She reaches up and presses the key into the circular depression on the vault door.

She can feel the bubbling excitement and anxiety filling the room.

From the key, a shimmering glow spreads across the vault door. Little vines of light creep outwards from the spinning heart, finding their way around the surface of the door. With searing vibrancy, they etch an image onto the door with arcs and corners and sharp angles.

Mara backs away as the lines of light spark and flare. The image on the vault takes shape. It's a map. It's a map of the The House of the Human. It doesn't have as much detail as the map she and Doctor Zhao looked at in his office. This map is more like a bold outline.

The map expands until it fills the vault door, and then, finally, the searing lines finish their movement, and the glow fades from the newly drawn image. But the door to the vault remains closed.

The Lady Banks pushes past Mara and examines the map.

Mara glances back at Auntie, whose expression is a mix of concern and curiosity.

The Lady Banks snaps her finger and L. Martin crosses over to her.

"Go get your gear," she tells him.

L. Martin nods with an evil smile and looks over at Auntie, sizing her up.

Mara feels her heart flutter. "No!" she shouts. "Wait!"

"That was a neat trick, but I don't see the point in waiting any longer," The Lady Banks snaps.

Doctor Zhao steps forward, raising a finger. "This drawing

is incomplete," he says, checking in with Auntie, who nods at him.

"Yes." Mara points. "See, it's missing an area right in the middle. What if going to the satellite was just about being able to see the whole house? See it from above."

The Lady Banks looks back at the drawing, at the section they're pointing to. "So what?" she says skeptically.

The map on the door is a layout of the house made of bold lines seared into the surface. Mara can see once again that it resembles a baby in a womb. Lines that she knows represent the rock wall and the thin moat form the outer border. Within those lines, the different sections of the house are indicated, but there are no buildings or any smaller details. To any normal person, it would look like a complete drawing. But Auntie, Doctor Zhao and Mara know better. Right in the center of the image where the baby's chest should be is a large open area.

Auntie says, "Mara, can you finish the drawing?"

"I'm not sure," Mara says. "But I have an idea."

The Lady Banks taps her wrist. "You better figure it out Mara. I was hoping for more than just a light show here." She walks back and joins her cronies.

"Go for it Mara," Sarah shouts encouragingly.

Doctor Zhao sets up a chair in front of the door for Mara to stand on.

"Okay," Mara says. She takes one last look at the drawing on the vault door. She lets her gaze take in the whole image. She doesn't know it, but she's using the eye of the artist, the gaze of the tracker. It's that soft listening state that all people enter when they look at the ocean, or a fire. It's the quiet mind of the visionary.

Mara pulls out her purple pencil from her front pocket and climbs onto the chair. She hopes her idea is a good one. Then she reaches up and boldly draws two arcing lines in the open space of the baby's chest. The two lines join at the top and the bottom forming the only thing that should ever fill a baby's chest—a heart.

The drawing bursts into dazzling light. Mara's bold beautiful heart brilliantly joins with the lines of the rest of the drawing.

And the vault door shudders.

Mara jumps down from the chair and hops away as it begins to move.

Weightless, smooth, heavy as the mountain, the vault door swings open.

Chapter 18: Revolution

What lies within?

The question sears the minds of the greedy Lady Banks and her cronies as the vault door swings slowly open.

What lies within?

The question bubbles in the hearts of Mara, Auntie, and their family as the vault door swings slowly open.

Its vast bulk moves in total silence, and creeps like a snail, inch by inch, as if it's hesitant and unwilling to open.

Within, a vast chamber is revealed. The floor, the walls and the roof are made of the same swirled copper and steel metal as the door itself. But there are no piles of treasure, no racks of weapons. There is only a single archway that stands solemnly in the center of the chamber. And even from where they stand outside, they all can see that the air within the archway shimmers magically, like a pool of oily water. And something is written across the top of the archway, but the writing is too fine to read from a distance.

The invaders push forward hungrily, but The Lady Banks stops them with her finger. "Everybody wait!"

She pushes Mara to the side and surveys the vault, making sure there's nothing hiding in the corners. Then she points at

Auntie and says. "After you."

Auntie takes Mara's hand and leads her and the rest of her family into the vault. Auntie heads them towards the archway, but L. Martin shouts, "No! Up against the wall!" Auntie jumps a little when he yells, startled, but she takes her family over to the side of the room. They line up against the wall there.

Mara's skin tingles with the tension in the room. Auntie's grip on her hand is rigid. Doctor Zhao's face is grim. Sarah looks fiercer than ever, and Kreak is doing his telltale anxious bobbing.

The Lady Banks and her cronies eagerly examine the archway. Mara can see their greedy looks, she can feel their scheming. She wishes she could have a close look at the archway herself. From where she's standing next to Auntie, it appears to be seamless with the floor, as if the pair of bronze and steel bars grew up from it, twisting as they rose until they bent towards each other and joined together. And she still can't see what the writing across the top says. The invaders are all discussing what the archway could be, but they're keeping their voices low.

Finally the Lady Banks turns towards Auntie and asks impatiently, "Well, what does it do?"

Auntie asks, "What does the archway say?"

The Lady Banks hesitates a moment, then looks up to the top of the archway and reads it aloud, "The Heart that Opens is the Heart that Shapes."

Auntie hears those words and Mara feels a glimmer of hope pass through her aunt.

L. Martin sneers, "Fru Fru garbage."

The Brother's K. nod. One of them adds, "This whole house is a pile of fru fru."

His brother laughs.

The Lady Banks cuts them off with a sweep of her hand. "Tell us what it does, Madame Designer."

Auntie shakes her head. "I honestly don't know. This is the first time I've been in here. As I told you before, the vault has always been closed."

"Lies." Grove coos.

The invaders simmer with impatience.

"Take a wild guess," The Lady Banks says.

Auntie raises her hand, then drops it. "Perhaps it's a portal of some kind? I have no clue where it would lead to though."

Ms. Pfiz nods, "This is what we think also."

Grove says greedily, "Perhaps to the real treasure?"

"Perhaps," Auntie says.

Mara can feel the invaders greed boiling. They edge closer and closer to the archway.

"Maybe to a room filled with weapons," L. Martin growls.

"Mmm..." Auntie sounds doubtful.

"What else could it be? Is it dangerous?" The Lady Banks asks Auntie.

"I honestly wish I knew more," Auntie says with a shrug.

Mara wishes she knew a way to stop these horrible people. She can tell Doctor Zhao's mind is racing also, but surprisingly,

Auntie seems curious.

The Lady Banks turns back towards the archway. She leans very close and examines the shimmering air within the archway. To Mara, it looks like a thin layer of water, gently undulating and iridescent like it has a sheen of oil.

One of The Brothers K reaches out and quickly touches the shimmering layer, which creates a ripple, like a pebble dropping into a pool. The Lady Banks furiously slaps his hand. "Noone touches it."

The brother recoils, surprised and angry. But then he looks at his finger.

"What'd it feel like?" his brother asks.

"Nothing really."

The Lady Banks is glaring at him, examining him.

He shrugs off the humiliation of getting slapped and says to her, "I'm ready to walk through. Just give me the word."

"No!" The Lady Banks snaps at him so sharply that he stumbles back a step. She turns away from him and looks at Auntie with a cold calculating expression on her face. For a hard moment the room is silent as she stares at Auntie. Then she says, "I'll be the one to open this portal."

Then without waiting another second, she turns and steps through the archway.

Her cronies push each other out of the way as they pile through after her.

Mara gasps in shock. Auntie's hand comes up to her heart.

The air in the archway boils and churns as the invaders splash through. There's a sparkling glow that lights up the room for just a moment, and a buzzing and a little tinkling of tiny bells.

The invaders spill through the archway, but instead of being teleported to some other place like everyone thought they would be, they pass right through the layer of shimmering air to the other side. And now they're just standing there, looking a bit confused.

The Lady Banks looks at her hands, then looks towards Auntie. Her cronies check themselves also, but nothing seems to have changed.

Auntie though, stares at them as if she's looking at a bunch of lab rats.

Mara feels a wave of emotions pass over her. It's like a tidal wave. It's so strong that she leans back against the wall. Her aunt glances down at her for a moment, then looks back at the invaders.

The Lady Banks and her cronies seem uncomfortable. Something is happening to them.

Ms. Pfiz speaks up first. "I feel weird."

They're all looking at each other, at their hands. Their expressions are changing rapidly. Frowns and smiles are smearing together. Growls and laughter are colliding in their throats.

"What is happening?" Grove calls out.

Mara thinks they actually look a little scared. The Lady Banks runs her hands over her face. The Brothers K are looking at each other intensely. Boheme Grove is swaying back and forth. She lets out an awkward giggle.

L. Martin seems to be boiling. He lets out a low long growl. The next moment he's laughing. They all seem to be torn back and forth between laughter and sadness, anger and joy.

The Lady Banks hisses, now with a dark look on her face, "I'm having feelingsssss..."

"I feel so much!" L. Martin roars.

Mara heart is pounding. They seem like they're gonna burst. She looks up at her aunt, who whispers back to her, "Watch, Mara."

The Lady Banks and her crew begin to move like they're in jello. Creeping and out of control, they laugh, they cry, they yell. They touch their faces and hands, they feel the air. Their eyes don't seem to see.

But then suddenly, L. Martin staggers a few steps, and his smile drops like a rock. "What is tha..What is that? Something...OW!" he suddenly screams and grabs his chest. "I'm being attacked!"

Mara's hand tightens around Aunties.

"Steady Mara," Auntie whispers.

L. Martin grabs his shoulder, then his chest. "I'm being attacked! Someone help me!"

Grove groans loudly and yells out, "I've been deceived!" She crumples to the ground. "Nothing but lies!"

The Brother's K. make horrible gurgling sounds. One of

them shouts, "I can't breathe!" The other hollers, "It's in my lungs, on my skin! GET IT OFF OF ME!" They contort into clawed tremblings. They beat their hands against their chests.

The Lady Banks and Ms Phiz too, crumble and gasp. They moan and writhe. All of them are drowning in some overwhelming wash of emotion.

"Auntie!" Mara cries out. It's too much for her, she can feel their suffering so clearly.

Auntie looks down at Mara and sees the tears in her niece's eye. Mara's eyes plead with her Aunt to do something, anything.

It's in that moment, seeing Mara share in the suffering of even their enemies, that Auntie realizes what the archway has done. Auntie whispers to herself, "The Heart that Opens is the Heart that Shapes."

Mara's heart, when she opened the vault door, shaped the effect of the archway. She shaped the archway so that those who pass through it would become imbued with empathy.

Auntie turns, filled with this new understanding, and she sweeps forward. "Quickly now!" She arcs around in front of the writhing invaders. From her robes, her own sketchbook and pencil appear in her hands. Auntie flashes the pencil across the page, and a chair materializes before her. She hides her book away again, turns, clears her skirts, and sits down.

"Stand back," she tells her family who have gathered behind her.

Auntie gazes out over the men and women before her.

Their cries have grown louder. They beat their bodies and tears bulge from their shocked eyes.

In a quiet, gentle voice Auntie speaks to them. "Come here," she says. She holds her arms out to them. "Come here, let me help you." Her words are so gentle.

The Lady Banks looks up first and tries to see through the film of pain that she's feeling.

"Look at me. Let me help you." Aunties words are warm.

L. Martin struggles to his knees and turns his head towards her.

The Lady Banks shifts towards Auntie's direction and wipes some of the tears from her eyes.

"Come here. I'm right here."

The Lady Banks stilts to her feet and shuffles haltingly towards Auntie, hands balled, shaking. Ms. Pfiz stands too now, her head drooping to the floor, eyes closed, body tense and trembling. She turns her head. She can almost hear.

"Let me help you." Auntie fills her words with love.

The invaders all begin to move towards her, on their feet, on their knees. They stumble, they crawl, they pull themselves hand over hand. Eyes pressed open, eyes pressed closed, moans and fight and struggle.

"I'm right here." Auntie's voice is a beacon.

As she comes close, Auntie's arm takes in The Lady Banks and pulls her to her side. The Lady Banks crumbles into her embrace.

L. Martin creeps closer, his hands grab at the air in front of him.

"I'll help you," Auntie says.

Grove crawls forward and clings to Auntie's knee. Auntie arms grow. They reach further to embrace Grove also.

Her arms stretch to bring in L. Martin. Longer, to cradle Ms. Pfiz, longer and longer, the two Brothers K.

"What do you feel?" Auntie whispers.

They speak over each other. "Helpless" "Pain!" "Poisoned!" "Robbed." "Lied to."

The Lady Banks whispers, "Enslaved."

"Used." L. Martin growls, "Beaten, abused."

Auntie says now, "Feel beyond the pain. What's there?"

The invaders do become calm in her arms. They settle and sniff.

"What's beyond the sorrow?" Auntie asks.

The frowns and strain fall away from the invader's faces.

"There's something warm," The Lady Banks finally says.

"It ripples," L. Martin adds.

"Is it laughter?" Grove asks.

"I feel that too now," Wall gasps.

"What is this? I've never felt this before," The Lady Banks asks.

After a moment, Auntie answers, "There's more. More than sadness, more than laughter. Feel deeper. Bigger than everything else. What's there?"

The invaders become quiet again. They listen. Eyes float, faces blend question and emotion.

"Oh my," The Lady Banks gasps. "Oh my, oh my."

"There's something," says L. Martin. "It's so vast."

"Vast and stable," Ms. Pfiz wonders.

Grove laughs, "It's as big as the Earth."

Auntie nods. "It is Earth," she says.

"Earth?" The Lady Banks whispers.

"Yes, Earth."

"It's so clear, it has shape and tone and color," The Lady Banks marvels. "I can feel it."

"This is Mara's gift to you all."

"The sadness, the laughter?"

"Your brothers and sisters in humanity. The world over. Their pain, their laughter, and their love are yours to share now. And Earth herself even," Auntie says. "You've been given the gift of empathy."

"Empathy," The Lady Banks whispers.

"Earth," L. Martin marvels.

"Their pain is our pain," The Lady Banks whispers.

"Their joy is our joy," Grove nods.

"We'll create peace," L. Martin offers.

"We'll bring health," Ms. Pfiz soothes.

"We'll spread bundance," The Lady Banks shares.

"A world of honesty and compassion," The Brother's K. say.

Grove whispers, "Everyone is included."

Auntie nods. She glances over her shoulder at Mara. She smiles at her niece in wonder, and in her heart, Auntie hears a song about children crying...

About how they grow...

How they'll learn so much more than their parents and their grandparents...

And about how the world is truly a wonderful place.

Epilogue

"Auntie, I… I don't really know what empathy is," Mara says quietly as she walks next to her aunt through a field of wildflowers.

"I know my dear. Empathy is when you can actually feel what other people are feeling. It's more than sympathy. It's having the courage to really share in other people's joy and sorrow," Auntie explains.

Mara crumples her face a little, then says "I think I understand what you mean."

"Your empathy is profound Mara. Think about how you always want to help people, like the boy on the island, or those rocketmen falling from the sky."

Mara is quiet for a bit. She really just wants everyone to get along. But it's true, she does seem to feel what other people are feeling.

Her aunt stops at a little purplish wildflower that has jagged red leaves and stems.

"What is that one? It's all over," Mara asks.

Auntie's eyes twinkle at Mara and the flower. "They're my love. They roam unhindered."

The afternoon sun dims, and the flare off the hillside meadow softens.

Auntie whispers to the small purple flowers, “Yes, thank you my beautiful ones.” She leans down and plucks a leaf, then hands it to Mara, “It’s called Dragon's Blood. Smell it's awkward scent, something earthy, iron... Or, maybe like blood.” She grins. ”Eat it.”

Mara laughs and then eats it. “It tastes like parsley.”

“Very tasty. They're a powerful healer.” Auntie’s gaze widens, and she sees the whole world as she looks down at this one small plant. With awe she says, “It heals your blood.”

Each day that passes, humanity heals itself, heals Earth. Mara’s heart, in shaping the effects of the archway, turned the bad people into good people. And this set in motion a chain reaction which swept across the surface of the world.

The Lady Banks convinced all of her evil partners to pass through the archway. Swaggering executives from the weapons industries fell into Auntie’s waiting arms. Oil barons, banksters, government cronies, food profiteers, insurance swindlers, all the most powerful of the self-serving ilk, they entered alone, vampiric, and insatiable. But they left together as the hopeful benefactors of the human family.

The changing tide took weeks, not years. The ammunition lines groaned to a halt. The abundance flooded from those who had hoarded it down to those most in need. The citizens of Earth awakened into this new age to feed and heal each other, to learn from and teach each other, to care for each other.

A new future, marked by a brilliant purple star.

"Auntie?" Mara asks, thinking about her art and feeling her doubts about herself crawling back. "Have you ever had an original idea?"

Auntie laughs. "Mara, I'm not sure if an original idea even exists." She kneels down in front of Mara and takes Mara's hands into her own. "The truest thing I've ever heard about artists is that the best of us are the greatest thieves. We steal any idea we can get our minds onto."

Mara giggles.

Auntie continues, "You have a great gift, but like we discussed, to use it well, you have to match your practice with great knowledge. I want you to try to avoid some of the mistakes I've made. So when you go back to class tomorrow, what are you going to do?"

Mara grins. "I'm gonna pay attention and learn everything I can."

"Why?"

"So that I know how to draw a parachute when I need to."

Auntie laughs. "Good. Though I do think creating huge marshmallows was a wonderfully *original* idea." She winks at Mara.

Mara's smile grows really big, and her heart beats so strong she can feel it against her sketchbook.

Auntie gives her hands a squeeze and then stands up and

steps away. She tilts her head and listens.

Night's stars brilliant, and the House of the Human.

Auntie slowly raises her hands to the sky and in her beautiful voice, she whispers,

"Oh World,

On this day and on every day,

May we learn to foster love and curiosity

For your Great Great Mystery"

CPSIA information can be obtained
at www.ICGtesting.com
Printed in the USA
LVHW081135250920
667103LV00017B/1541

9 781735 266039